THE G〔...〕RUPTOR

Alex Martin was born in the USA in 1953 of a Greek mother and an English father. He was brought up in Kent and educated at Winchester and Cambridge. After a short time in theatre and film production, he became a teacher, working in schools and youth clubs in Kent and London. He recently spent five years teaching English in Italy. His previous writings include two children's books, *Boris the Tomato* (1984) and *Snow on the Stinker* (1988).

The General Interruptor

ALEX MARTIN

PENGUIN BOOKS

PENGUIN BOOKS

Published by the Penguin Group
27 Wrights Lane, London W8 5TZ, England
Viking Penguin Inc., 40 West 23rd Street, New York, New York 10010, USA
Penguin Books Australia Ltd, Ringwood, Victoria, Australia
Penguin Books Canada Ltd, 2801 John Street, Markham, Ontario, Canada L3R 1B4
Penguin Books (NZ) Ltd, 182–190 Wairau Road, Auckland 10, New Zealand

Penguin Books Ltd, Registered Offices: Harmondsworth, Middlesex, England

First published by Viking 1989
Published in Penguin Books 1990
1 3 5 7 9 10 8 6 4 2

Made and printed in Great Britain by
Richard Clay Ltd, Bungay, Suffolk

For Hugh and Paola Ward-Perkins

Ubi bene, ibi patria

1984

**Saturday
7**

So this is Pandoro. A very pretty town: piazzas, fountains, cafés in the sun. Just what was required.

There are houses with frescos painted right across their façades: muscly men reclining under the eaves while naked girls serve them drinks (nice work if you can get it). Beneath the houses, a vegetable market. The stallholders don't spiel like they do in England. Just stand there looking earthy and cunning. Between them weave lip-sticked ladies on high heels, clicking like bits of bone china. Very right and proper-looking. On the street corners, outside the banks, rotund financiers jabber at each other with emphatic gesticulations. Then, once in a while, a vast orange bus comes wheezing past, wipes out whole tableaux, like a curtain on a stage.

I arrived here by accident, meaning to go to Venice, only I got sick on the train. Not surprising really, if you consider the bill of fare of the night before. One fat, glistening frankfurter, purchased from a Turkish gentleman at Munich station; four mackerel and mayonnaise sand-wiches; one runny tomato, punctured by unknown object in rucksack; 6 oz. Danish blue cheese with pulverized digestive biscuits; one orange; one squidgy banana; numerous cans of beer; one miniature bottle Johnny Walker; ditto of Famous Grouse; one large hunk of Christmas cake (gift from Sarah); one thermos lukewarm coffee. All of this was joggled around in my gastric juice for eight hours or so, until something inside me waved the flag of rebellion and the entire repast came thundering incontinently out, hitting the station platform of Pandoro around three and a half seconds before I did.

Some of this vile decoction splattered the trousers and shoes of His Serene Majesty the Station-master of Pandoro. Making him instantly less Serene, and consider-ably less Majestic. Fortunately there is no law in Italy against vomiting on people, otherwise I am certain I should now be serving a crushing sentence in gaol. As it was, the man had to satisfy himself with a withering glare of disgust, from which I scuttled hastily away, grateful to have been spared my life.

A nurse in the First Aid room made me lie down, and I stared at a white ceiling for maybe twenty minutes, until I got so bored I decided that even staggering around feeling sick was better than this, so I got up and left, grabbed a bus into town, and sat down to breakfast in a piazza on brandy and black coffee. When this stayed down, I packed in a couple of croissants and a cappuccino. His lordship my stomach accepted.

I've decided to stay a few days, but finding a room turns out to be difficult. There is some kind of trade fair on 'meat technology' in progress, so the hotels are full. A three-hour trudge leads me finally to the Pensione Rosa, where there is only one room left: a dark, dank box, none too clean or comfortable, with a view of a dripping grey wall outside. It smells like a second-hand sock emporium. For the moment this will have to do.

Sunday 8

Wet, clinging fog all day. Church bells in the morning, the silence of the tomb thereafter.

Bought a map and a guidebook and sat in a café all afternoon, reading about how the noble Roman city of 'Pandaurum' was taken by the Visigoths, then the Ostrogoths, then the Franks, then was subject to our old friend 'warring factions', with rival barons cutting each other's noses and ears off, until the Venetians came and stopped them. The Venetians ruled for 400 years, bringing peace and economic exploitation, only to be ousted by Monsieur Napoléon Bonaparte, who bloodily crushed a rebellion, stole some paintings, and demolished a Roman arch before going on to higher things elsewhere; there was more fighting, the Austrians took over, then there was Garibaldi and the Unification of Italy, and they all lived happily ever after – except for the 'dark period of Fascism', which was brought to an unceremonious end by a rain of Allied bombs. These destroyed a number of civic monuments (since 'accurately restored'), but unfortunately missed the Pensione Rosa.

The city attracts me. I get an intangible but very strong feeling of living in the past here. More genuinely and more bizarrely than in Venice, which is a gigantic cliché by now, let's face it (though not bad as clichés go). I think I'll see about getting some work. I can always move on if I don't like it.

A piece of luck. I breezed into the Buckingham School of English, asked to speak to the director of studies, and found myself in the presence of this somewhat limp-looking specimen who claims to have met me at Oxford. Stephen Gold. Of course I couldn't remember him from a piece of cheese, but he rescued me from my amnesia by recounting that I was extremely drunk at the time.

'Ah, well, that explains it,' I said. 'Whole months of my university career are swallowed up in the blackest alcoholic oblivion.'

'You sang "The Chastity Belt", I remember.'

'Really?'

'Yes. With gestures. It was killingly funny.'

'Pleased to hear it.'

'I met my future wife that same evening. It was your song that brought us together, in a strange kind of way.'

'How romantic.'

He grinned. 'Happy days, eh, Paul? Student life . . .' He sighed, and poured out a predictable list of sentimental high-spots − breakfast at George's café, May morning under Magdalen tower, the clanging of Great Tom, Eights Week, debates at the Union, and so forth, while I just sat there and thought, only the English could have such a crass conversation.

When his nostalgia had spent itself, and I'd added my two-penn'orth of how I remembered nothing but hang-overs, he asked me what I was doing in Pandoro.

'I'm looking for work,' I said.

'Ah.' His face clouded. 'Have you got a qualification in Teaching English As A Foreign Language?'

'Yes, I have. Just done it in London.'

I was about to add that I considered it the biggest load of balls I had ever had the misfortune to be exposed to, but wisely kept this to myself.

'Good.' He was smiling again. 'That's a good start. But

have you got any experience?'

'Erm, no.'

His face clouded again. 'Oh.' He looked down at an anal collection of pencils on his desk. 'Well, I'm afraid it's our policy not to employ people without experience at the Buckingham School . . . You'd have to go to one of the, erm, lower-quality schools and put in some time there first.'

'Right,' I said, 'I won't hang around. I'll see you when I've got some experience.'

'Wait a moment,' he said. 'You wouldn't happen to be free this evening, would you?'

'I could be. Why?'

'I need someone to cover a couple of lessons for me . . . Paid, of course.'

'I haven't gained any more experience since five minutes ago.'

'Never mind that. It's a three-hour stretch, six to nine. Can you make it?'

I said I could, and that was that. At the end of the evening I was given thirty thousand lire. They felt good, those crisp bills in my pocket. For nothing, really. Chatting to two groups of perfectly pleasant people about holidays and cars. And I've been asked back tomorrow.

I've worked every day this week — hence no diary. Covering for a girl called Jane, who's got the flu. Long live the virus!

The school's not a bad place. Friendly staff, with a solid core of after-hours drinkers. There's talk of forming a football team. Could be a painless way of working off some of the booze and pasta kilos which seem to be gathering about my waist like sycophants round a millionaire.

**Saturday
14**

Another somewhat depressing weekend. The people at the school are all off on mysterious private expeditions of their own, to Verona, Milan, Venice, etc. I assume the aim is amorous – or at least sexual – from the guardedness of their replies.

My students are all off to 'she'. This confused me at first. Who – or what – is 'she'? *'In montagna!'* they vociferously explain. I'm still stumped. Then someone – an obliging young fellow called Carlo – stands up and demonstrates. He crouches in the middle of the floor as if to defecate, thrusts his fists out to the sides, and begins weaving right and left. It turns out he's skiing. The Italian word is *'sci'*, pronounced 'she'. *'Sciare.'* *'Andiamo a sciare in montagna.'* Sounds so elegant and effortless.

No 'she' for me, though. In any sense of the word.

A cautionary tale. Last night I took advantage of the derisory cost of wine to get a skinful in a pizzeria. Staggered home in the fog, and woke up feeling as if someone had driven an axe through the back of my head, the blade being twisted to prise the cleft further open whenever I attempted to move a limb. Aargh! What the hell do they put in their plonk? Petrol? Pulverized tarmac? Cordite? Or perhaps some hideous, mutation-inducing pesticide? Never, in all my years of boozing, through many a daring encounter with Algerian bin-ends and tongue-shrivelling Bulgarian rosé, have I had such horrific after-effects.

By noon, with plenteous *acqua minerale*, a hot bath (three thousand lire extra), and aspirin, I felt well enough to go out. Just. The sun seared the backs of my eyeballs, but I forged on. People were out in the streets, all in their churchy Sunday best, carrying neat parcels of pastries home for lunch. They have this very staid walk, processional in style, one arm stiffly devoted to the spouse, the other to the pastries. Staid and a little smug. 'Look at me, observe my smart clothes, my wife's fur coat, our polished shoes. We've been to church. We've been to the pastry-shop. And now we're going home for lunch. We do this every week. We do things right . . .' Behind them trot their kids in patent-leather pumps, bored and overdressed.

The weather is good, the air warm. I notice, in the square, a number of attractive and apparently unattached women, hanging around in groups or sitting in cafés in twos. Dressed to the nines, of course. High heels, stockings, tight skirts, lipstick, furs. Hair in a cloud of coiffured artifice. Razor-sharp make-up. Some amazing bodies. They seem ageless from sixteen to forty.

I wonder, though, do they *go*?

Wednesday 18 Jane came back to work today, so my teaching and cash flow cease. Met her briefly. She has red hair and grey eyes, an unusual combination which I would not have expected to like but do. The eyes search you, draw you out. Very haunting.

Professionally, my prospects seem good. I checked out the Somerville School, run by two extremely gay gentlemen from Brighton who've practically forgotten how to speak English but welcomed me with open arms; and a grim outfit called the Madison Institute, where students are force-fed 'business English' through tape recorders and given points every time they get something right. Both need casual labour. Both also want 'experience', but with seven days at the Buckingham under my belt I feel I tell no lie in saying yes to this. They pay a bit less than the Buckingham, but less is a whole lot better than nothing.

The other (potential) good news is that they're looking for a new language teacher at the university. Interviews Friday week.

I scrape together a curriculum vitae on a borrowed typewriter. While wrestling with such tortured existential questions as whether eight months driving an Interflora van in Wolverhampton makes me a more or less appetizing proposition as a university language teacher, there comes a knock on the door, and this young Senegalese woman who has the room next door (shared, it would seem, by about thirty-five relatives who are all in the digital watch and carved elephant trade) is standing there in a *very* loose gown – beneath which she is apparently nude – asking me if I have any aspirins. She has a *'mal de tête'*, her drawling voice tells me, while the long limbs beneath the robe are full of languid invitation.

'I have no aspirin,' I tell her, 'but I have this', and show her a bottle of Scotch.

'OK.'

She gets to the point very quickly, taking only a sip of Scotch before putting the glass down on the table and letting the gown slide from her shoulders. Her body has an extraordinary sheen to it, as if she's dipped herself in oil. Doubts and confusion assail me, but it's too potent a case of Opportunity Knocks to do anything but submit.

'Afterwards', as they say, I asked her in a dutiful sort of way whether she wanted anything, meaning more Scotch, a cigarette, etc.

'Forty thousand lire,' she said without batting an eyelid.

'What?'

She repeated the figure, worth about twenty pounds. I was a little taken aback. I had assumed this to be a strictly amateur contest, with no prize money for either side. But in the end I gave it to her, with only a flicker of resentment. It can't be much fun being professionally rogered all day long. Specially when you consider the grisly types who probably make up her usual clientele. I'm no Johnny Weissmuller myself, but in the absence of a bald pate, sagging hair-matted tits and a lurching pot-belly, I should think I was the high point of her working week.

Still, twenty pounds for half an hour sure beats my fifteen pounds for three hours. Perhaps I should become a prostitute.

After this encounter I felt strangely glamorous. Invulnerable, like Achilles fresh-dipped in the Styx. I tried briefly to return to my c.v., but it seemed utterly stupid and banal. So I downed a swift Scotch as I dressed, and, with a cigarette dangling from my lips, sauntered down into the street feeling bright and spry as Cock-a-doodle-dandy.

Working on the (admittedly rather bestial) theory that the smell of success turns women on – just as the smell of failure turns them off – it occurred to me to pop round and see Jane.

By great good fortune she was in.

'Hello, Jane,' I said (always a great original when it comes to opening lines).

'Oh, hello, um . . . Tom, is it?'

'Paul.'

'Right! Paul . . .'

'I was wondering if you fancied coming out for a pizza.'

She didn't answer for a bit. 'A pizza? . . . No, I don't think I can. Not tonight.'

'OK. Perhaps another time, then?'

Again a short silence. 'D'you want to come up for a drink?'

'Yeah, sure. That would be nice.'

'Come on, then.'

After three flights of gloomy stairs, she welcomed me into a massive, dark, and ancient flat that seemed to have

been hewn out of solid rock. The floor was covered in cracked, uneven tiles, a death-trap to the slouchers of this world. The place was full of junk.

She showed me into the kitchen, where an onion was lying half sliced on a chopping board in the centre of the table.

'I was just making supper,' she said.

'Oh yes? What's on the menu tonight?'

'Tortellini with ham, cream, and peas.'

'What's the onion for? Dessert?'

'No,' she laughed, 'for the peas.'

'Tell me the recipe.'

'Are you interested in cooking, then?'

'Very. I prefer eating, of course, but since you can't have one without the other –'

'Quite. Well, this is nothing – a piece of cake . . .' She smiled at the awkwardness of her expression, the light catching her eyes most prettily. She picked up the onion. 'You just slice one of these, very finely, then fry it gently in butter until it's soft.'

She was looking great. I wanted to tell her, do something silly – like grabbing her right there among the onions. But then I thought no, wait.

'And what do you do next?' I asked.

She rested her gaze upon me once again. 'What would you do next?' she asked. Our eyes met. There was something there, I knew it – and she knew it too.

'I think I'd . . .'

A shadow crossed her eyes.

There was a sound of keys and a lock turning in another part of the flat. Footsteps approached. Heavy ones, entering the room.

'Hello, Bill,' she said.

I turned and saw a stockily built red-faced man with a grizzled black beard, a sweat-strewn forehead, and hunted eyes.

'This is Bill,' said Jane.

'Hi, Bill.'

His mouth twitched in acknowledgement. 'Who are you?'

'I'm Paul.'

'Oh.' He lit a cigarette, then turned to Jane. 'I spoke to that prat at the insurance office again, but they won't do it. The only insurance they'll do on a bike is for damage *you* do to other people. Fat lot of bloody good that is.'

'Have you tried anywhere else?'

'I rang Generali, but they said I'd have to go in to discuss it. Usual stupid response. *"Non possiamo dare queste informazioni per telefono."* Idiots. Anyone would think this was still the bloody nineteenth century! I'm giving up on this, I tell you. I've had it up to here. And I've got better things to do with my time. Like earning money . . .' He cast a belligerent eye about the kitchen. 'Any wine open?'

'I don't know. Have a look in the fridge.'

'I'll just dump my papers in the office.'

He turned, and I saw his hunched shoulders disappear from the room.

'I think I'd better go,' I said.

'As you like,' said Jane. 'It's not a problem. Stay for a drink if you want.'

Bill reappeared, went straight to the fridge, and pulled out a bottle of white wine, which he rapidly uncorked.

'Drink?' he inquired.

'Yes, please.'

He poured three glasses and handed them round. 'You a teacher?'

'Yes,' I said.

'Hm! Join the crowd.'

He drained his glass and refilled it. 'What's cooking?'.

'Tortellini,' said Jane.

'Fresh?'

'Yes.'

'Good. Can't stand the packet ones.' He turned to me. 'You staying to eat?'

'Erm, no . . . no, I've got somewhere to go.'

'OK.'

'Are you a teacher too?' I asked.

'Unfortunately,' he said, and belched: a loud, proud, clattering, metallic salvo.

'Bill!' cried Jane.

'Scuse me,' he said, without a hint of apology in his voice.

I asked if he taught in a school.

'No.'

'University?'

'No, God help us.'

'Privately?'

'Yeah. Business groups.'

'Ah. Interesting?'

'No. Extremely dull. But' – he rubbed his thumb and index finger together – 'lucrative.'

I finished my wine. 'Thanks for the drink,' I said. 'I'd better be off now.'

'Where are you going?'

'Erm . . . well, nowhere as a matter of fact.'

'Stay for dinner! It's cold out there.'

I stayed.

As I groped my way down the stairs in the small hours, pissed as a newt, I reflected that, slightly weird as they were, I quite liked them both.

Met Mike Shipton, the school cynic, in a bar (Da Marco – very pleasant, English beer on draught – served cold, which is a bit odd, but not bad once you get used to it – juke-box, good atmosphere). Asked him about the personal life of Jane. He gave a bitter laugh.

'Ha! What personal life?'

'She lives with this bloke Bill, right?'

'If you can call it living.'

'What's he like?'

'Burnt out.'

'He seemed nice enough to me.'

Mike shrugged. 'I don't know him very well. Just seen him loping round the streets, looking like death warmed up. People say he works twenty-six hours a day.'

'I don't understand it. A pretty girl like her . . .'

'Yeah, we've all asked ourselves that. They're just a couple of limpets, stuck on the same rock. Nothing'll budge them.'

'Are they lovers?'

Another bitter laugh. 'Do they look it?'

'No, I admit, but . . .'

'I suppose there may once have been a brief passionate fling, before he got his beer-gut and betting-shop look, but that would have been a very, very long time ago.'

'Why do they stick together?'

'I don't know. Used to the smell?'

I said I found this a little sad, and Mike said I'd find plenty more sadness here if I stayed around.

'So why do you stay?'

'I don't know.' He sighed. 'Inertia, laziness . . . also, I suppose, I've known worse. The good thing about Pandoro is, it's not an evil place. It may not be much good, but at least it's not evil.'

JANUARY

**Monday
23**

Mike and his girlfriend took me 'she-ing' yesterday. Spectacular mountain scenery, only an hour from town. We did cross-country, which the Italians call *fondo*. Frustrating but fun. Fell over five times just getting out of the car park. Then wobbled and slithered round the six-kilometre track, unintentionally doing the splits several times and adopting a number of the more challenging yoga positions. I had frequent, embarrassing collisions with other skiers, knocking drinks or sandwiches out of their hands as they took a rest at what they thought was a safe distance from the piste, and dug endless handfuls of gritty snow out of my shoes, gloves, and underpants. Yet, in spite of all, it was somehow exhilarating. Got back too bushed to do anything but eat and crash out – at nine.

Looking back, the day's outing was most interesting sociologically. You leave the city at eight in the morning, and the roads are packed with a Sunday rush-hour of cars with skis strapped to their roofs, crammed with people in their multicoloured ski-suits, all smoking and gesticulating and rubbing sleep out of their eyes as they roar up the motorway to the north. Most of them, says Mike, are going downhill skiing, and indeed we pass a resort on the way up with coaches disgorging hundreds of space-invader-type figures in grotesque plastic boots on to the waiting areas by the ski-lifts. There is something of the Gadarene swine in all this, people bursting out of the confinement of cities to hurl themselves in demonic droves down mountainsides. I suppose there's a desire for freedom and contact with nature behind all this – or possibly the hope that they'll break a leg and get some time off work.

The *fondo* track was much less crowded, though here I note the extraordinary Italian gift for *a uniform for every occasion*. Mike and I are, in time-honoured British fashion, togged out in a ragbag of old jeans, misshapen sweaters and silly woollen hats, while Mike's girlfriend, Flavia – and everyone else on the track – wears a special one-piece shiny nylon '*fondo* suit' – a sort of heavy-duty leotard with tights, all with colour-matching gloves, long white socks, and little rucksacks on their backs. No wonder Mussolini was such a hit in this country, with his parades and fancy regalia for all and sundry. Still, mustn't complain. They're a very sociable lot. Had several friendly conversations with total strangers *en passant*. They treat you in a very relaxed way. It seems they aren't *afraid* of each other, the way we Brits are.

**Tuesday
24**

Today the first shots are fired in what promises to be a long battle with bureaucracy. This was my morning:

1. Went to an office called the *Anagrafe* – sort of a municipal registry – to apply for *residenza*. This is not a residence permit, just a piece of official paper stating that you live in a place. Why you should need this is beyond me, but I'm assured that it's essential. In order to get it you have to fill in a form. And in order to get the form you have to stand in a queue. This I did, outside an unmarked yellow door, for forty-five minutes. When I was finally admitted, I was told that this was the wrong door. A further twenty minutes outside a subtly different (but also unmarked) yellow door, and I got in. A bilious type behind a desk asked me what I wanted. 'A form,' I said. He shoved one at me, and pointed to the door.

Question: why are these forms not freely available for the public to take? Why must they be kept behind mysterious doors, guarded by bored and truculent civil servants? Is the aim simply to inconvenience the public? Or, by inventing unnecessary work, to create jobs for unemployable people?

2. Coffee break. I puzzled over the form in a bar. Most of it was fairly clear, but it became obscure – as all good forms do – towards the end. I put it away and consulted my list of other tasks.

3. The *Ufficio Stranieri*. The so-called 'Foreigners' Office' of the *Questura*, which is one of the many mysterious branches of the police. This, I have been warned, is no fun. Here I needed to get a *permesso di soggiorno*, which *is* a residence permit, and even more essential than the *residenza*. More waiting, this time on hard metal chairs in a grey-walled room. There were three desks in the room.

At one sat a young man in a sweater, typing extremely slowly. At another a bulky, grey-haired man in a resplendent blue uniform with flashes of purple and gold. He would make a good Latin American dictator. The third desk was empty.

While I waited, a French girl was cross-examined by the man in uniform. His questions got progressively more insulting. Why do you want to stay in Pandoro? Are you really a student? Or is that just an excuse? Can't you study in France? You've got a boyfriend, is that it? Does he live in Pandoro? Have you got another boyfriend in France? Do you like Italian men? They are strong, eh? Hot-blooded! And so on. She trembled and meekly replied. I would be tempted to spit in his face. Yet, when my turn came, I found myself being meek too. The power of a desk and a uniform!

The dictator was not interested in me. Not in my sex life, anyway. I asked him what documents I needed for the *permesso*, and with a very bored expression he told me: my passport, a letter from my employer, a certificate of medical insurance, a letter from me requesting the *permesso*, and three regulation-sized photographs. I made a list under his impatient eye, then left.

The letter from my employer will be tricky. I must think about this. I must also find a flat. The Pensione Rosa is getting me down.

Friday 27

Interview at the university. When I was called in, I found three Italian professors seated behind a long desk. One beamed at me with immense goodwill (it turned out he didn't speak a word of English and was there to make up the legal minimum of three), another shook hands indifferently and then stared out of the window for practically the whole of the interview, and the third welcomed me, fussed, chattered, grinned, roared with laughter at obscure jokes of his own making, and told me how much they like people who (a) are 'fresh and raring to go', and (b) have plenty of spare-time interests. My van-driving experience went down a bomb. 'Ah yes, and it

was in Wolverhampton! Well, well, that's interesting. Enoch Powell territory. His old stamping-ground, rather. A very brilliant man, but hoist with his own petard. Now, a course on British racism would be a marvellous thing. From *Othello* to the National Front. Could you do that? Or the geography of the British Isles? The Hebrides, the West Country, the Midlands, the Yorkshire dales, the Highlands, East Anglia, Cumberland, the Fens? So many Italians think London is England and England is Britain, which is absurd. Courses in literature are useless without a knowledge of landscape and local history. How can you understand John Clare unless you have hiked through Northamptonshire? – as I have, by the way, and very wet but rewarding it was too, with just a few pennies in my pocket and an old Ordnance Survey map, and nothing but the hedgerow birds for company. I have always wanted to write a book about topography and literature, but like everything else it's a question of time. And then there is British cooking, which – contrary to foreign opinion – is very rich and various. The wonderful Norfolk hams and Lancashire black puddings, sides of smoked bacon hanging in butchers' shops, legs of lamb, beef dripping, suet, steamed puddings – ah, jam roly-poly! What a fantastic invention! The perfect antidote to a pea-souper fog! – treacle tart, baked apples with custard, those splendid dense black fruit-cakes soaked in Jamaica Rum, bangers and mash, eel pies, Frank Cooper's Oxford Marmalade, spotted dick, bread and butter pudding, roast beef and two veg, pork chops with apple sauce, sherry trifle, Stone's Ginger Wine, Paterson's shortbread, haggis and neeps, fish and chips wrapped up in the *Daily Herald*, rhubarb crumble, hot cross buns . . .'

While he kept this up, I politely listened, the beaming professor fell asleep, and the third alternated between the window and a doodle of great complexity to which he would add in brief ferocious bursts before noisily throwing down his pen and burying his head in his hands. Meanwhile my questioner continued: '. . . but, of course, our students should know something of British popular culture too, Max Miller and the world of the saucy postcard, Morecambe and Wise, the *Goon Show*, Vera Lynn, *Punch*, Heath Robinson, Andy Capp, Bud Flanagan and the Crazy Gang, the Black and White Minstrels, Marie Lloyd, Billy Smart's Circus, Blackpool Pier, *Hancock's Half Hour*, Sid James, Bruce Forsyth, Tommy Steele, Giles, Val Doonican, James Bond . . .' There was no stopping him.

After maybe fifteen more minutes of this manic tour of

the jumbled encyclopedia of his brain, the professor suddenly broke off and said, 'Well, that's quite enough of that. Now, have *you* got any questions you would like to ask *us*?'

I walked back feeling dazed and not a little depressed, consoling myself with a couple of beers in a bar along the way.

When I got back to the dreaded pensione around ten, there was a message for me to ring Professor Ferruzzi (he of the topography and cuisine). I did so, and the extraordinary fellow offered me the job.

I've had three hectic weeks, the like of which I would not wish even on a sworn enemy. At the cost of much exasperation and rage, interspersed with episodes of seraphic patience, I have seen through to a happy conclusion (or am on the brink of doing so) three essential tasks: rental of a flat, plugging myself into the local bureaucracy, and my first serious taste of work. Today I pause for breath, wondering what hit me.

Following the local custom of advertising one's need for accommodation in the newspaper, I was telephoned by a woman with a whining neurotic voice, whose name – translated literally – means 'Cat-eater'. First impressions suggest this may be hideously appropriate. She is utterly mad. She showed me round a horrible, poky room with one tiny window that didn't open, no kitchen, and a toilet that you could only reach by a perilous journey through an icy attic. I told her this would not do.

'But you're a student, aren't you?' she asked.

'No, I'm not. But even if I was, I would still want a bathroom.'

'Oh,' she said. 'Well, I usually rent this room to students.' She seemed to think this somehow answered my point, as if the word 'student' meant the same as 'animal'.

So I repeated, 'I'm not a student. In fact I'm a teacher at the university.' I used the word *'professore'*.

It was as if a bomb had dropped. Her manner instantly changed. 'Oh, *professore*! I'm so sorry, *professore*! I thought . . . no, no, my mistake . . . I'm sorry, *professore*!' and so on, wittering and whining and hopping about. She then revealed that she had something *much* more *'signorile'* (i.e. posh).

This sounded a great deal better, and indeed it was – a light and spacious flat on the fourth floor, with two

bedrooms and a balcony, and the various necessities of life provided for without having to call in caterers or set out on risky expeditions with torch and overcoat.

I asked her how much it cost, but before she would tell me, she decided an interrogation was necessary. 'You won't have guests, will you? Because this is a flat for one person. And you won't give private lessons? Because it's a residential block. And you won't use the furniture in the lounge? Because it's antique. And you won't do too much cooking in the kitchen? Because it's new. And you won't get *residenza* in Pandoro? Because I only rent to non-residents. And you won't tell anyone you rented this from me? Because I don't want people pestering me. And you will polish the floors every week, won't you? And clean the windows? And shut the shutters whenever you go out? And water the plants on the balcony? And wax the furniture? And you haven't got a girlfriend, have you? Because I know that trick of asking for a flat for one and then bringing in a secret lover, I know that trick very well . . .'

I gave her all the assurances she wanted, with no intention of being bound by any of it. We agreed on a price and after an extremely fussy contract-signing session – during which my passport and birth certificate were taken out and photocopied – I was given the keys.

A couple of evenings later I noticed a man in a trilby and raincoat hanging around in the shadows outside the block of flats. There was something decidedly sinister about him.

I was just letting myself in (one eye over my shoulder) when he called out, 'Signor Zmeet!'

I turned. 'Sì?'

He hurried up and introduced himself – as Mr Cat-eater – then produced one of the photocopied pages from my passport. 'You are English, aren't you?' he said with a searching look.

'Yes . . .'

'Can you please tell me why you have got "Petersburg" written in your passport? Petersburg is in Russia.'

I pointed out that the word he was looking at was in fact Peterborough, a city in England famous for the issue of passports, and a very different kettle of fish from St Petersburg, the old capital of tsarist Russia.

He looked mystified.

'In any case,' I added, 'St Petersburg has for the past sixty years been known as Leningrad.'

'Oh yes?' he said, his eyes flinty with suspicion. 'And how do you know that?'

At this point I exploded. 'Everyone knows that! At least everyone who isn't a complete ignoramus! And if you don't believe me, I suggest you buy an atlas and look it up. Or telephone the British Embassy in Rome. Or the Soviet Embassy for all I care.'

For a moment he held his ground. 'I thought you might be Russian,' he said.

'Well I'm not! Russians don't have British passports! And I'll thank you to learn a bit of geography before you come creeping up on me out of the shadows again!'

Then he crumbled. 'I'm sorry, *professore*,' he said, 'very sorry', and began an elaborate dance of retreat, doffing his hat repeatedly, and muttering apologetically, '*Mi scusi, professore, mi scusi. Ho sbagliato. Pietroburgo. Mi scusi. Mi scusi. Mi scusi . . .*' And so faded away, as if drawn by a string into the darkness.

Shortly after this I managed to get my *residenza* and *permesso di soggiorno*. This involved so much queuing, grovelling, arguing, toing and froing with documents, forms, photographs, letters, notarized translations, authenticated signatures and photocopies that I groan even to think of it and prefer to forget the whole thing as fast as possible. I emerge from the experience with a strong determination never to enter the nightmare world of Italian bureaucracy again, except (a) at gunpoint, (b) on business of the utmost urgency.

Then there were the university exams. Oh boy. In Britain, as I recall, these are solemn and even terrifying occasions, conducted with icy rigour by gaunt, Gestapo-style invigilators whose black eyes seem to bore through space and be able to detect a speck of dust out of place at 300 metres. Sessions are timed to the second, and a shuffling foot or discreet cough rings out like a pistol shot in the tense hush of concentrating minds. In Italy – at least in Pandoro – you have the feeling of being at a horse fair, or possibly a Mafia open day.

The exam papers are very faint, almost illegible stencilled sheets, usually with the ends of lines missing, and richly stocked with typing errors. Students are invited to respond to such challenging essay topics as 'Define coffee' and to supply the missing words in sentences like the following:

1. Human life is nasty, brutish and _____.
2. A _____ in time saves nine.
3. Go to work on an _____.

Throughout the exam teachers and professors talk in loud voices to each other about what they did at the weekend or about which of the female candidates have the nicest tits. Meanwhile the students cheat. This (apparently sacrosanct) activity takes many forms: copying from other students' papers, consulting grammars or dictionaries hidden in billowing sweaters, or, if all else fails, asking the invigilators for the answers. For women, large floppy handbags provide a convenient receptacle for forbidden books, and tops that fall forward to reveal a vista of bra-less breasts can be very effective when asking examiners for help. For men, things are a little harder, though a motorcycling jacket with twenty or thirty zipped pockets clearly came in very handy, as did a large sports bag containing 'football kit' with such essential footballing items as *The Oxford Advanced Learner's Dictionary of English.* One man hit on the brilliantly effective idea of not washing or brushing his teeth for several months before the exam, with the result that he sat in a kind of charmed circle of smell, which no one dared to enter, and where he was free to behave as he pleased, like some strange pirate king.

Once the papers were in, we had the grim task of marking them. My initial amusement at efforts such as 'I have never eaten a Chinese plate' or 'The coffee is not hard enough' turns to boredom, frustration, and – ultimately – pity. There seem to be very large numbers of students who, after seven or even ten years of defining coffee and filling in gaps in sentences, will get a degree in English without the slightest notion of how the language works. My heart goes out to them. They are being sold short.

After a couple of days of sun, the weather has turned foul. A strangling fog, laden with exhaust fumes and the exhalations of factories and central-heating plant, hangs in the streets like a pestilence. The cold (it goes down to minus 19 at night) is vicious and cuts through to your bones. The locals, I note, wear heavy woollen trousers and sheepskin jackets. Hats too. I feel naked in jeans and nylon bomber jacket, though these always did me in Britain. As soon as my first pay cheque comes, I shall go and buy heavily into animal skins. Meanwhile I huddle indoors, prepare lessons, and fire off a salvo of letters home.

By far the most difficult to write is the obligatory letter to Sarah. To keep the record (and my thoughts) straight, I note down the gist of our conversation the night before I left. We were in a rat-hole of a so-called 'French bistro' (complete with Venezuelan waiters) in Covent Garden. A candle burned between us as we struggled to finish a bottle of sour wine.

SARAH: I'm sorry to say this, because I don't like repeating myself, but I think you're making a big mistake. You're walking out on your future.

ME: What future?

SARAH: Your job, your prospects. And [*a reproving look*] me . . .

ME: I've already explained about all of those. My job was driving me bananas. There's only so much interest to be squeezed out of building trade directories, and I reached that point well over a year ago. Anyway I've quit now. There's no going back.

SARAH: The editor's job was there for the asking.

ME: But I didn't want it! How often do I have to say that? Now, leaving *you* is a different question. You know I don't want to do that. That's why I'd like you to come with me.

SARAH: Oh Paul! What the hell would I want to do that for?

ME: For every decent reason under the sun. For the sake of us, some fun, a change – God knows, life itself! For the sake of not thinking permanently in terms of 'career moves'.

SARAH: That, Paul, is precisely your trouble. You are incapable of thinking in terms of career moves. With predictable results. Look at you. Twenty-nine and nowhere in life.

ME [*poisonously*]: That depends very much on how you define 'nowhere'.

SARAH: What's that supposed to mean?

ME: Let's look at you. You've got somewhere, right?

SARAH: I like to think so.

ME: You're twenty-eight –

SARAH: Twenty-seven.

ME: OK, twenty-seven. But you look more like thirty-seven.

SARAH: Thank you *very* much!

ME: I mean it, Sarah. You've got bags under your eyes that would do credit to a person of fifty, your skin's pale and unhealthy, and your mind – your soul, the jewel of your being – is locked away in a narrow and meaningless little dungeon of stupid social conventions – impressing people at dinner parties, having expensive lunches, reading the right crappy books, wearing ghastly French shoes and middle-aged clothes, complaining about the mortgage and the price of Volvos – things that have bugger-all to do with living and just keep you prisoner.

SARAH [*coldly*]: If you really think that's what I'm like . . .

ME: I'm telling you that *is* what you're like. And I hate to see it, because I know you've got something better inside you, which, if you only gave it the chance, would come flaming out and let you burgeon and blossom in the most magnificent way.

SARAH: And what about my job? Perhaps you've forgotten that it's my salary that's been paying for the flat, the weekends away, the little luxuries . . .

ME: Take a year off.

SARAH: I can't.

ME: Ask your boss.

SARAH: I can't.

ME: Of course you can.

SARAH: I can't, Paul, I can't!

ME: What harm would it do? He could always say no.

SARAH: Paul, you are so bloody UNREAL sometimes! Do you have *any idea* how many bright young solicitors there are waiting in the wings, just dying to have a go at a job like mine? If I drop out now, I'll find my job taken and I can wave goodbye to a partnership until my late forties at the very least!

ME: So you won't come.

SARAH: No.

ME: That's that, then . . . Will you come and see me at least?

SARAH: That would be very nice.

I tried to pay for the meal, but Sarah would have none of it, plonking her Diners Club card proudly on the bill before I could get to the crumpled fivers in my pocket. 'Keep your money,' she said. 'God knows when you'll next have a job.'

Sarah and I are very different people. That is a fact which must be faced. Yet in spite of our disagreements, she knows in her heart that I'm right when I attack the streamlined emptiness of her existence, just as I know she's right when she points out the shapelessness of mine. We feed, in a way, on our differences.

Through the business of writing her a letter, then thinking about past times, she seems almost to be here in the room with me. I'm sorry she isn't. I'm working my way through a bottle of Ballantine's, and would dearly like to be doing it with her. It's sad drinking alone and remembering. Yet it sometimes gives you the truth in a way that nothing else can. Perhaps what we had (and still have?) was 'love' after all. Perhaps it still is. I don't know, but I'm starting to realize that it's not to be thrown carelessly away.

Rooting around in a second-hand bookstore, I came across one of those old favourites, long out of print, which you find only once every ten years, and in the most unlikely places: Viktor Ubriakov's *La Cuisine érotique*, first published in a clandestine edition in (yes) St Petersburg in 1888, and courageously reissued by Pernichon of Paris in 1926. It's one of the few truly successful erotic texts in existence; and it's practical too. Basically a recipe for aphrodisiac dinners, it is also a great hymn to the beauty of the female body. Flick through it and you find *Vagin de Pommes Walewska, Culottes en Tourbillon, Tétons de Melon en Belle Vue, Poulet en Chemise Déchirée, Asperges Droit de Seigneur, Mousse au Chocolat 'Seins de Négresse', Bœuf Soixante-neuf . . .* It's great to have it around again. I lent my original copy to a prick of an art critic, who of course never returned it.

In the afternoon we played football. Mike, Denis, and Wayne from the school, Bill (of Jane and Bill), myself, and four Italians. We used half the pitch and played England versus Italy, with kitbags for goals. Despite inferior numbers, the Italians triumphed 12–3. *Che vergogna!* Their feet were like lightning. They'd fiddle around for ages, weaving complicated patterns around us and themselves, and then, just when we were getting impatient, suddenly flash out a searing (and invariably accurate) shot at goal. Our only resource was what they call *il pressing nordico*, i.e. chucking ourselves bodily at them and trying to knock them over. But they were too nimble, and we ended up covered in mud and no glory. Still, it was all played in a good spirit, and in the obligatory 'third half' at Da Marco, as we replaced in beer what we'd lost in sweat, we all agreed that a good thrash around a football field is about the finest thing there is. 'Especially if you've got a hangover,' said Bill, his face fiery with exertion. 'Best cure I know.'

With drunken optimism we decided to form a proper team, and discussed the colour of the strip, possible names, etc. 'The Pandoro Petomanes' was one suggestion from Bill. 'The Pink Panthers' was another. I rather fancied 'Aston Villa', on the grounds that we might get invited to play teams like Juventus and Anderlecht by mistake.

'I don't think we'd fool anyone for long,' said Mike, and I said the real Aston Villa didn't fool anyone for long either. Denis said, 'Do you mind, I'm from Birmingham', at which we all expressed our sympathy and said we'd never have noticed if he hadn't told us, he looked perfectly normal, etc. This got him riled, which goaded us into a new bout of mockery (we were on our seventh or eighth round of beers by now), until it was obvious that he was getting genuinely upset. Bill changed the subject, but

Mike, who can't resist a put-down, carried on making barbed remarks in a poor imitation of a Brum accent – which was actually closer to Bradford – and we could see Denis was not enjoying them.

Now Denis is one of nature's pre-ordained victims. Gangly, uncoordinated, with a turnip-shaped head, a floppy, wet mouth, and eyes that seem to float too loosely in their sockets. He dresses the part too, with green Terylene trousers that flap round his ankles a good three inches above his shoes, a range of mustard, olive, and raw-sausage-coloured shirts, and a shapeless maroon sweater that hangs off him like a curtain. In Britain you'd scarcely notice him, of course, but here, where physiques are compact and they dress to kill, he sticks out a mile. After a few pints his face looks even slacker and more disjointed than usual.

Mike continued to dig. 'Now what would the man in the street in Birmingham have to say about this? Eh? Can you give us some gritty West Midlands wisdom?'

Denis, who had been doing his best to ignore him, now turned and rested a damp but steady gaze on Mike, and said, 'You know, Mike, I used to laugh at your mockeries of other people, until it dawned on me that what you said about them behind their backs you wouldn't hesitate to say about me behind mine. And indeed it turns out you call me "the Fish" when I'm not around. That has an unfortunate physical appropriateness which I would be the first to acknowledge, and no doubt many people find it amusing. But ever since I was a child, when I had the chance to study the subject at leisure, I've found that this essentially cruel style of humour is an absolutely infallible sign of weakness and emotional insecurity in the people who practise it. You provide a shining example yourself. What you're really doing when you mock someone is looking for approval and confirmation of your own worth as a human being. Being emotionally stunted and congenitally mean, you're incapable of gaining this approval through acts of generosity, kindness, affection, and so on, so you take the nearest alternative, which is cutting down someone else. Purveying hate, basically, instead of love. A very crude strategy, which often backfires, but surprisingly common. Now I shouldn't think any of this interests you, not in its finer points anyway, but I thought you might like to know that, besides finding your remarks painful and offensive, I also find them extremely revealing, of a very feeble and mean-spirited personality desperately seeking attention, with nothing to offer the outside world except a few cheap laughs.'

Denis paused, looked round the table, and said, 'Gentlemen, I wish you all a very good night.' With that he stood up, put some money on the table for his drinks, and, leaving a fresh pint untouched, walked out.

All eyes turned to Mike. He had a word for most situations, but something told us he was going to have difficulty making light of this one. He sat still, looking pale and crushed, his eyes fixed on the door.

At last he moved, reaching out a hand to his glass and taking a long thoughtful draught.

'Well, Mike,' said Bill, 'how does it feel to be emotionally stunted and congenitally mean? Or was it congenitally stunted and emotionally mean?'

Mike's mouth curled. 'Pompous prat,' he muttered. 'I did psychology at teacher-training college too.'

I'm becoming more and more aware that when you move to a new city – even if you think of it as simply a place on a map, with buildings and streets, and roads leading out to a particular sort of country – what really makes it what it is, the thing that shapes your experiences, is the people who live there.

What's more, they're not just individuals and families getting on with their lives, which is what you tend to think at first. There are factions too – groups set out in patterns of alliance and opposition, like pieces on a chess-board. Or rather on hundreds of chess-boards, with hundreds of games being played all the time. And where people don't find a game to their liking, they set up one of their own.

Mike and Denis have just done this. And they want their friends to take sides. This is something I do not wish to do, since it's a petty quarrel, as pointless as it is venomous. They no longer speak to each other, not even at work. Messages have to be passed via third parties. Mike – whom I consider to be entirely in the wrong and simply nursing his injured pride – insists on my allegiance and support. I've told him he's being vain and a twat, but he won't listen. There's something very childish about him – Denis is right. But then being right isn't everything either, and when it comes to which one I'd rather spend an evening with, I'd choose Mike every time, because he's so much more entertaining. The stupid thing is, both of them suffer by their hostility. It does neither of them the slightest bit of good, yet they think about it all the time, their lives are ruled by it, and they think everyone else's should be too. Along with others I try to make peace occasionally, but they don't want to know. It seems they need their little conflict like a drug.

Last night another conflict arose, and about this one I can't be so detached, since I'm directly involved.

Around seven o'clock Bill's girlfriend, Jane, rang up out of the blue to say, 'How about that pizza you promised me?' I hadn't seen her since the night I went round for a drink, except to say hello in the street, so this came as a bit of a surprise, but I said OK. Bill was away in Treviso, she said, interpreting at a big-deal conference on pesticides, so she was at a loose end. But just *how* loose I didn't realize until after the meal when she invited me back for coffee and grappa and let me know in a thousand unspoken ways that she was, well, aching for it.

A month ago this wouldn't have been a problem. But now I've come to regard Bill as a friend and, much as I find Jane sexy and mysterious, I'm sufficiently in control of my rampant hormones not to throw away a friendship for the sake of an hour's bouncing up and down on a bed. So I was frank with her and said I could never look Bill in the eye again if I made love with her. Her response to this was to laugh. She said they didn't have that kind of relationship, they were each free to do as they pleased.

Now I've been spun that line before. I've even spun it myself. And it's crap. People are jealous. They don't live together for nothing.

I said, 'No, Jane, I'm sorry', and made a rapid exit before she could get to work on me again; or, perhaps more importantly, before I could weaken.

But Jane is a determined girl. When I got home, she was there ahead of me – having the advantage of a bicycle – not the slightest bit put out by my sudden departure, smiling and saying I was creating imaginary obstacles and there was absolutely no problem, and – her very words – 'I want you, Paul. Now.'

'And I want you, don't get me wrong, Jane. It's just that I –'

But there was no stopping her. She had my hand in her dress before you could say Swiss Family Robinson, and

I'm ashamed to say my resolve just vanished like a conjuror's rabbit, and we stumbled and fumbled our way into the lift, kissing and touching and getting more and more excited, until we somehow got into my flat without disturbing the neighbours, and there we tore off our clothes and . . . well, the rest is obvious.

Only it wasn't totally obvious. It was wonderful. We were at it for three hours, and still hungry for more. I even forgot to feel guilty.

But now, twenty-four hours later, even as I think (with extreme pleasure) of what we did, I'm wondering what on earth I shall say to Bill.

Saturday 3

Saw Bill at football. Guilt boiling inside me. But he said nothing, acted perfectly normally. I assume (and pray) Jane hasn't told him.

As we sat in Marco's bar, discussing whether it would be possible to get beer on an intravenous drip, I watched Bill talking and laughing, and getting redder and drunker and more outrageous, and I thought, I don't want to hurt this guy, I really don't. Only of course it was a stupid time to think it; I should have thought it when I was outside my flat with Jane. But still, I thought, something might be saved if I act now. Better late than never.

So I won't see Jane again. I mustn't.

The problem is, it's going to be difficult, because she stays in my thoughts. That night we shared was more than just fun. We felt good together, felt right. When we talked, it wasn't that polite stuff over breakfast when you find out with a sinking feeling that you have nothing in common and don't even fancy each other any more; with us it was real. We wanted more of each other. 'Let's meet again,' she said. 'Soon.' And I said yes, and meant it.

So how the hell do I say, 'Let's *not* meet again'?

Or should I just let things drift?

After work this evening I managed to kidnap Jane for half an hour's serious talk. We went into a dark corner of a bar and I told her there could never be a repeat of last Thursday.

'Oh?' she said. 'What happened last Thursday?'

'That was the night we . . . you know . . .'

Her brow puckered. 'Was it? I can never remember these things.'

'Yes, it was. And I wanted to say I'll remember it all my life – even if you've already forgotten it after a week.'

'I haven't forgotten it. It's just that I'd forgotten the exact day . . . I remember very clearly. It was fun.'

'Yes, it was fun. It was more than that. It was absolutely marvellous. But in a way, you see, that's precisely the problem. We mustn't get involved.'

'I quite agree.'

'It would hurt Bill terribly.'

'Yes.'

'And we'd end up hurting ourselves too.'

'Would we?'

'Yes. I'm sure we would.'

She shrugged her shoulders. I had a suspicion she wasn't giving this business her full attention.

'Jane,' I said, 'this is very important. It hurts me to say this, because I feel we got very close that night, but we've got to stop, here and now. We've absolutely got to.'

Jane sat very calmly smoking and resting her grey eyes on me. She looked almost amused. This angered me.

'Are you the slightest bit interested in what I'm saying?' I asked.

She smiled, as if she had some secret knowledge of the business of which I was unaware. 'Yes, Paul, I am interested. But I think you're exaggerating. There's no need for all this . . . tragedy, is there? We had some fun; but if you don't want to do it again, that's OK by me. It's a free planet. I'm happy either way.'

This was not what I wanted to hear. I had come prepared for a sacrifice, and this easy indifference of hers threw me right out of step. 'It's a free planet' indeed!

'Was it really that . . . that *ordinary* for you?' I asked. She looked puzzled.

'Was it ordinary for you?' I repeated. 'Do you often make love with people you hardly know, and reach such . . . such passion? . . . Such heights of –'

'That is a very rude question,' she said.

'No, it isn't. At least it's not meant to be. It's –'

'It *is* a rude question. I don't discuss things like that.'

'Look, Jane,' I said. 'I can't handle this! One moment you're talking about making love as if it was, I don't know, a game of squash or something – easy come, easy go, take it or leave it – and the next you're all prissy and defensive like a Victorian schoolmistress. I mean what is your real opinion about this? What's your position?'

She twisted her lip, and appeared, for the first time that evening, to concentrate.

'I haven't got a position,' she said.

'What does that mean?'

'It means I haven't got a position! I'm me, and you're you, and I just do what I feel like doing, and I don't like having to explain and justify myself to other people.'

'I'm just trying to understand you.'

'But you haven't asked if I want to be understood.'

'Well, do you?'

'No.'

And that was that.

So – I've done my painful duty, and I don't feel the slightest bit better for it. I just feel like a fool. I made a great sweat and pother out of nothing. What's worse, I don't even understand what was said. Is Jane really so cool about everything? Does she really live on impulse? And, if she does, is this the result of long and careful thought about the problems of existence, similar to the enlightenment achieved by Buddhist monks after endless years of training, or is she simply thick-skinned?

Whatever my answers to these questions (and for the moment I have none), I am forced to admit that I am more curious about her than ever. And with my curiosity goes a damn great whack of straight sexual attraction. I fancy her still like crazy. Possession has not rid me of desire.

Thursday 8   Alone with Jane in the staffroom for five minutes after lunch. Offered her a coffee from the machine. Coldly she said no thanks, and went to get one for herself. That would seem to seal the matter, for the time being at least.

Settling down to a routine at a school, you begin to notice that every class has a personality of its own. Some are slow and steady achievers, others slow and steady non-achievers; some are jolly, some are glum; and some are just plain horrible – flash, impatient know-it-alls who want quick results and end up bored, aggressive, and learning nothing.

Last night at the Buckingham I had my dreadful 'Thursday at Eight' class. A pharmacist, a lawyer, three extremely posh housewives, a lady doctor of wondrous

Friday 23

beauty and stupidity, a travel agent, and a policeman. All of them, except the last, have Money – very large and conspicuous heaps of it – and a commensurate dose of poisonously overbearing self-confidence. They are hopeless students. They can't understand why English doesn't just stick to them the way wealth does, and they resent any attempt to make them study or think. They particularly dislike English idioms which can't be translated word for word into Italian – things like 'We've run out of milk' or 'You'll have to put up with it'. In fact, I've come to the conclusion that they hate the entire English language – because, I suspect, it's outside them, beyond their control, something they must adapt themselves to, rather than a thing to be bought, claimed, and stuck up on the living-room shelf for the world to admire.

The one exception to all this is the cop, Aldo, whose humble origins and job make him simultaneously the class underdog and scapegoat – a very demanding role. He is snubbed for his clothes (cheap, lacking in designer labels), his provincial accent, and above all for the fact that he represents the State – that arch-fiend and Beelzebub, issuer of parking tickets, tax forms, rent laws, and a million other impediments to the enjoyment of life. Meanwhile, of course, the man's courtesy and quiet intelligence go completely unnoticed.

I decided to give this bunch a shot of culture. Photocopied Blake's poem 'O Rose, thou art sick!' and shoved it at them. Apart from pronouncing 'the invisible worm' as 'the invisible warm', they seemed to take it on board without too much difficulty.

Then I asked them to discuss what it might possibly mean. What is the rose? What the worm? And so on. There was silence. Each pupil looked more embarrassed than the next.

I asked Stefano, the lawyer, who has opinions about everything. He frowned, sighed, and explained that as he didn't know anything about '*questo William Black*', the social conditions under which he was brought up, the philosophy of the time, etc., he did not feel qualified to hazard an opinion. The others vigorously agreed. Impossible to discuss without more information.

All right, I said, never mind the 'right' answer, make a guess. What does it mean to you? They all frowned and stared blankly back at me.

'Well, look, is it a poem about gardening? Or is the rose a symbol of something else?'

Finally, out of the silence, Aldo hesitantly volunteered that the rose could be the city of Pandoro, 'so beautiful, so rich', and the worm *la malavita*, the criminals, prostitutes, and drug addicts that infest her shady places. Great cries of 'No!' and the 'discussion' (i.e. Aldo-bashing) began in earnest. He was accused of reading too many newspapers, of inexperience, political bias, ignorance, naïvety, disproportion. He went carefully through the facts. Pandoro is well known to be a crossroads of crime, he said, with drugs worth hundreds of millions of lire being traded daily, the Mafia and the *Calabresi* making serious inroads into the city's commercial and political life, underworld murders committed 'punctually' every month in the southern suburbs, the area around the railway station 'a sea of organized prostitution', judicial inquiries thwarted at every step, and so on. He had seen it all, he said, with his own eyes.

'*Deformazione professionale!*' came the triumphant reply – he was clearly over-impressed by what he saw at work and failed to take the more ample perspective necessary in such debates. The leader of the ample perspective-ists was the chemist, Dr Silvestro Sbovolone, his hairy hands flying in and out like a squeeze-box player's as he spluttered angrily about the great marble and electrical industries of Pandoro, the trade fairs, the Chamber of Commerce, the university ('a second Harvard'), the School of Tourism, the Museum of Agriculture and Taxidermy, the Roman amphitheatre, the Philharmonic Orchestra, the duomo with its famous frescos ('if not by Giotto then certainly by one of his followers'), the great beacon of Catholicism represented by the Sanctuary of the Madonna of Pandoro, not to mention the innumerable centuries of 'cultural and economic primacy in Europe'.

Aldo conceded all this, while admitting his ignorance of the historical and cultural side of things, but stuck to his basic point. The chemist threw up his hands and said there was no point talking if one left culture and history out of account. Stefano backed him up with a decisive '*La cultura è fondamentale*', and Aldo, heavily outnumbered and outbludgeoned, bowed out. '*Non dico più niente.*'

The matter was sealed by Valentina, a great edifice of lipstick, jewellery and hairdressing, who told us how she had once spent a year in Milan, and it was *much* worse there, really terrible, with all the skyscrapers, the traffic, the stress – and the prices in the shops! *Ma guarda, una follia!* For her, Pandoro was the best city in Italy. Everyone noisily agreed. The truth had been established. Someone pointed out that it was past nine o'clock, and the class dispersed in a flurry of overcoats and handbags. Aldo looked trampled and downcast.

I took him out for a beer to restore his flagging spirits, but the poor fellow was beyond therapy. The stuffing had gone out of him. The mob had won. There is no worm in the rose. *Buona notte, William Black.*

I'm taking advantage of the Easter break to get in some skiing in the Dolomites, and – since there's a blizzard going on outside – to sit down and catch up on my neglected diary. I need to get some things off my chest.

First, I have to say that working at the university gets me down. This I have come to realize from the fact that (a) I get a headache the moment I walk in there, and (b) a feeling of lightness and joy comes over me the moment I walk out. If I try to analyse what it is precisely that 'breaks my balls', as they say here, I would pin it down to two things: inefficiency and corruption.

If you want to get, say, a photocopy, you have to go into a tiny office on the third floor, which is occupied by one of those special institutional demons who can be found in offices all over the world, carrying out their life's mission of putting obstacles in the way of innocent people. They are particularly common in education for some reason, perhaps because the business world no longer has time for them, perhaps because here they see fertile ground for their proliferation. I'm convinced that they're bred in a great international pound – perhaps run by Gabbitas & Thring – behind barbed wire somewhere in East Germany. I envision couples of them mating with weird bureaucratic rituals among piles of dusty chits, forms, and registers, their *coitus* continually *interruptus* by telephones ringing and timid knocks on the door. 'Can't you see we're mating!' they cry, 'Go away!' and they get back to it with a sigh as footsteps retreat sadly down the corridor . . . Pandoro's Obstructor-General is a man of exceptional power, a veritable baron; his office is a bottleneck for all paperwork, including the post, passing into, out of, and through the university. No one gets a bit of paper but by him. His name is Signor Cotogna – Mr Quince – and the fire of his nostrils is terrible.

I would love to see his job description. It must be a

million pages long. He seems to shoulder the entire administration of the university, from the purchase of toilet-rolls to the annual accounts. So he's always busy, run off his feet. You must approach him apologetically, flatter him, wheedle his attention away from the twelve jobs he happens to be doing when you come in, crack a couple of jokes about how he's the only person in Italy who does any work, and, while he's still smiling, bung in your request with precision and style. Often you're competing with a host of rival pilgrims to his shrine: encrusted old professors who have devoted a lifetime to the art of queue-barging, brash young lecturers with machine-gun mouths firing sixty words a second, and middle-aged department heads in clouds of perfume and furs whose lipsticked mouths carry a permanent smile of pure poison. There's a whole parade of possibilities, people either toadying or arrogant, but no one behaving normally or with the slightest regard for dignity.

Teaching is a job for arseholes. This is the effective motto of the place. Anybody who tries to do it in anything but the classic manner of standing up in front of a class and droning for an hour is a double arsehole. You want to photocopy a little poem? A racy article? An interesting picture? Forget it. It'll take you anything from an hour to a whole week to get it done, and in the end no one will thank you for it. In fact you'll be labelled a 'Stakhanovite', a holier-than-thou creep who's trying to get popular with his students and show up his colleagues.

And then, of course, everyone's on the fiddle. The professors give a heroic lead here, defying the law and just about every ethical principle you can think of for the sake of ease, profit, and prestige. Standard practices are: running a private school with parallel courses to those at the university, not showing up for lessons, spending half the year on 'study trips' abroad, getting students to write books for you, using grants to set up vanity presses where your friends and associates can publish drivelling monographs which no decent publisher would touch with a barge-pole, rigging appointments committees so as to give jobs to your protégés, forcing students to buy your books, do your research, parrot your opinions, lick your boots . . . the varieties are practically endless. In this uplifting moral atmosphere it is scarcely surprising that students approach the whole business of getting a degree with the utmost cynicism. Apart from cheating, they will use bribery, sex, intimidation, sycophancy, tears, or even straight offensiveness to get through their exams. The idea of actually *studying* anything doesn't seem to enter their heads. Instead they memorize photocopies of other people's lecture notes. 'It's the only way to pass exams,' one girl told me. 'You must repeat only what the professor has said in his lessons. Nothing else.'

'What about forming your own opinions?'

'Oh yes, you can do that. As long as they are the same as the professor's . . .'

The system is rotten. It stinks. Individual talent is strangled at birth. The place is a cloning machine, churning out cynical, mediocre minds by the truckload.

There are, thank God, the exceptions. The occasional bright-eyed student whose natural gifts and optimism miraculously survive their five-year bludgeoning at the hands of the 'educators'. Even Ferruzzi. He's neither ignorant nor corrupt, and openly despises those who are. But of course this puts him out on a limb, and he's so busy hating everything about the place – and being hated in return – that he can scarcely bear to set foot in it. He rushes in, does his bare minimum of hours, and rushes out again.

The philosophy of survival is the only one that works.

'Shut up and think of your pay cheque.' This is what I try to do, but I feel a spineless wretch doing it.

As a change from all this, and to earn a bit more money, I've been teaching regularly at the Buckingham School, filling in for people with flu or that other well-known disease, 'the white week' (i.e. skiing in the mountains). I almost feel like one of the staff now – and the chameleon Stephen Gold has never dared mention 'experience' again.

In spite of having practically two jobs, I get plenty of free time, which I fill with books, sport, food, drink, and the occasional bedroom adventure – though not again with Jane. I've been reading Byron's letters, full of similar exploits (at a somewhat higher social level). His scenes of the opera and social gatherings in Venice, midnight trysts on the banks of canals, amours, feintings, escapades, swimming, riding, and learning Armenian – of all things – in the Monastery of St Lazarus, give a feeling of a wonderful lost age, when life was there for the seizing and not a dreary matter of 'finding a career and sticking to it'.

Mind you, being a lord, poet, and international celebrity probably has its advantages in any age.

The football team has gone from strength to strength. With the improvement in the weather, more and more people have been turning up, and recently we have played all eleven-a-side games. England still gets beaten by Italy pretty regularly, but the margins of defeat have been narrowed. We even scored a victory one week. An unusual feeling, being British and winning.

The third half also flourishes, varying in length from two to five hours, largely according to whether Bill is there to conduct operations or not. I have come to notice, though, that it's the Brits who sustain the bulk of the alcoholic input; our Italian friends will have one or maybe two beers, then switch to Coke or other horrors. They don't drink to get smashed like we do. In fact they carefully avoid it. The only true native piss-artists you see are the old men who sit in bars playing cards. Their noses start glowing around ten in the morning, and stay that way till midnight. But they're from another age – the wild and hopeless Italy of Mussolini. And while they quietly drink themselves to death in the back streets, a new, rich land is growing up around them, with technology, supermarkets, fancy financial dealing, Fiat Unos, and holidays for all. You have to *hunt* to find someone poorly dressed, or driving a car more than three years old. Britain seems mouldering and backward by comparison. And in Britain, as I remember, *everyone* is on the booze, all ages and classes, not just the old and clapped out.

The other great feature of expatriate life in Pandoro, the Mike–Denis war, has dragged on for a month or so, with hatred sitting in the school staffroom like a cloud. But then, just a few days ago, Denis went off to Trieste for an interview at the university, and to everyone's immense surprise got offered a job there, starting straight after

Easter. The owner of the Buckingham, Mrs Carpaccio, threw a great howling wobbly at the news, and refused to pay him his retirement bonus (which amounted to over a thousand pounds) because he'd not given the required notice. However, since they'd found a replacement almost immediately, this struck everyone as a very false argument, and it was decided that Denis must be supported even if it meant going on strike.

I was in the staffroom when this decision was conveyed to Mrs Carpaccio, and she positively exploded into the room and began screeching about things called the *scala mobile, anzianità, paga base, una tantum, il contratto nazionale, l'accordo con i sindacati*, and a swarm of other bewildering technicalities, which had the desired effect of leaving all the teachers bamboozled and not knowing their arses from their elbows. Sensing triumph, Mrs Carpaccio let them swelter for a few moments in their ignorance and, with a smug smile cracking her make-up from side to side, said, 'So you see I really *can't* pay Denis his bonus, even though I would like to.' She took off her little gold half-moon glasses which she used for arguing, and stood up to go.

Denis looked downcast, and the other teachers sat biting their lips and looking at the floor, but Mike suddenly said, in a very matter-of-fact voice, 'So we go on strike, then.' I'll never forget the way Mrs Carpaccio just froze in mid-step at the word 'strike'. She very slowly turned round and, with fury visibly rising in her face, strode up to Mike and started yelling at him as if she were trying to knock him over with her voice.

Mike took it all without flinching and, when she had shouted herself hoarse, said quietly that the period of notice was in the contract as a protection for the school management, not as a means of tricking the teachers out of their rights, and since the school already had a replacement for Denis, it was a question of principle now, and he would not personally teach another lesson until Denis had been paid in full.

'All right, you can go too!' said Mrs Carpaccio. 'I don't want troublemakers here.'

But Mike said, 'You know perfectly well you can't fire people for standing up for their colleagues' rights.'

'Just watch me!' snapped Mrs Carpaccio, and marched out.

Then Denis came up to Mike and said, 'I appreciate what you're doing for me, Mike, but I don't want you to lose your —'

'I'm not doing it for you,' said Mike.

'Well who the hell are you doing it for?'

'For all of us. If we let her get away with tricking us once, there'll be no stopping her. She'll be at it permanently from now on.'

Stephen Gold, who'd come scurrying out of his office at the sound of raised voices, now joined in the discussion to say that he was sure the management always acted in good faith, there had never been any cause for complaint, legally their position was watertight, and so on, until Mike just said, 'Don't be such a drip, Stephen', and led the teachers in a turbulent mob to Mrs Carpaccio's office.

She said there was nothing further to discuss; when Mike said there was, she accused them of trespassing in her room and threatened to call the *Carabinieri*. Then Wayne said if Mike was fired, they would all stop work and the school would be paralysed until he was reinstated and Denis received his bonus. Mrs Carpaccio exploded again, and fulminated about trade unionism and the collapse of civilization, and finally said to Denis, 'Oh, take your money and go.'

Afterwards, in the bar, Denis stood us all a round of beers and thanked Mike with obvious sincerity. Mike, not snide for once – perhaps because he was the hero of the moment and felt he could afford a grand gesture –' accepted his thanks and said he was glad he'd been able to help. No mention was made of their old quarrel, but reading between the lines you could see they were both very relieved to have found a way of burying it without a word being said.

1985

**Monday
12**

A little over a year after arriving in Italy, I'm on my way home. There's a two-hour delay on my flight, so in the palatial comfort of a plastic seat in Pandoro airport I'm taking the opportunity to fill a yawning gap in my diary.

I note that I've written nothing since Easter last year. Probably because the novelty of life abroad has started wearing off. But also because not much has happened, and I've had a crisis of conscience about the whole business anyway. Why do I bother writing a diary? Will I, or anyone else, ever read it? If not, what on earth can be the point? An act of communication requires two people,

a speaker and a listener. If I'm the speaker, who is my listener? Me, again.

I remember it was a history master at school, 'Shagger' Welsh (of the beautiful and, by repute, insatiable wife), who got me interested in diaries. 'The text for this term is the *Memoirs of the Duc de Saint-Simon*' — here he gave a special little grunt that he used to punctuate and dramatize his sentences — 'an account, probably based on diaries, of life at the court of Louis XIV. Now I don't know if any of you are in the admirable habit of (grunt) keeping a diary . . .' 'The admirable habit'. The words stuck in my mind. I can never think of diaries without also thinking 'admirable habit'. It's a clear case of conditioning. Very irritating. Like a bit of my brain that belongs to someone else. Would Shagger have pronounced those words so lightly had he known the power they would have? I suspect he would. Being a historian, and dedicated to primary sources, it's logical to try and generate a few for future colleagues to work on. Perhaps in 300 years there'll be schoolboys reading this, looking up words like 'airport' and 'plastic' in the notes, and thinking how squalidly colourful life used to be in the far-off twentieth century.

I can't pretend to have solved my crisis. It happens that I now feel like bunging down a few thoughts whereas I didn't before. So here goes. Schoolboys of the twenty-third century, watch out.

The heat this summer has been monstrous. As extreme in its brooding sultriness as the cold was cutting and vile in winter. Just sitting still, you find sweat squirting from you. Only the thinnest cotton clothes are tolerable. I'm going home to cool off, as much as anything.

What report will I give of life here to those who ask? It's hard to know. The good and the bad are so finely mixed that they're practically inseparable. Take the incredible inefficiency, for example. The university prospectus published at the *end* of the academic year instead of the beginning (when it might have been of some use); letters taking three weeks to travel ten miles; the lack of reliable information on practically any subject you care to mention. This kind of thing is extremely irritating, yet it has its positive side: people don't rush you, they're tolerant of mistakes and delays, and always ready to make the best of a bad lot. *'Pazienza!'* they say. 'Things will work out.'

Or take the business of *bella figura*. (This does not mean, incidentally, that Italians simply like to 'look good'. It's a much more extreme thing, amounting to an entire philosophy of life, namely that looking good is *all* you should worry about, and forget the rest.) You see this cult of appearances – and neglect of substance – in every moment and walk of life, from their farcical politics to their unjustly celebrated shoes. It's all beautifully, artistically engineered to create just a moment's impression, nothing more. After that it disintegrates. I feel like I'm living inside a giant firework.

And yet – I have to admit – it somehow continues to charm. Not only that, but the fact that people go to immense trouble to look smart, even if they're only going out to buy a newspaper or a bit of *prosciutto crudo*, is a sign of extraordinary *optimism*. Blind, silly, superficial, call it what you will, yet it's an expression of enormous faith in life, and in society. For an Italian there's always someone out there to look good for, so they make the effort. My attitude – the British attitude – of saying, 'It doesn't matter' is basically an admission of defeat.

The prevailing philosophy is hedonism. You work (as little as possible) in order to live, and the purpose of life is pleasure. They don't mess about with concepts like 'being of use to society' or even 'being a good citizen', and they don't put hard work, ulcers, and social status on a pedestal like we do. If people choose to bust a gut getting rich, or helping the poor, that's fine, it's their business. The great majority prefer to trundle along, having fun where they can, and be left in peace.

They have a natural distaste for violence, and an instinctive love of beauty, which is as close as many of them come to having a morality. This shouldn't work, but somehow it does. The young are not aggressive or drunk, the middle-aged not depressed or intolerant, and the old do not live in fear. I think, on balance, that they have more to teach us than we have to teach them.

The effect of the Italian way of life on a fresh, strait-laced, and puritanical Anglo-Saxon can be devastating. Some go rigid and absurdly British, clinging punctiliously to the ways and manners of their abandoned homeland, whereas others go 'native' in style, becoming caricature Italians, dedicating themselves wholly to being shambolic and pleasure-seeking, vague, deceitful, permanently late and confused about times and places, lazy, inefficient, and sly. What a 'healthy' response might be is anyone's guess. Somewhere in between, I suppose – a kind of mildly accommodating hybrid.

I can't help thinking of Rocco Sigorski in this context. His mother's Italian, his father Polish, and he was brought up in Connecticut. Just before his eighteenth birthday he decided he preferred wandering in Europe to being hunted in Vietnam. He's lived in France, Portugal, and Italy for a total of fifteen years, eight of them in Pandoro. He won't budge now. His language is an arresting personal hotch-potch of Italian and English, mixing vocabulary and grammatical structures from the two with surreal ease. How anyone who speaks only one of these languages can understand him is a mystery to me. The first time I met him was when he turned up on the football field. He played in glasses, crumpled linen trousers, and an old pair of soft leather shoes. He scored a lovely goal, twisting in a long, angled shot from just short of the corner flag, and I was curious to know who this gifted newcomer might be.

He said he was an artist.

'What kind of work do you do?'

'I paint, *quadri* and stuff, you know, *acquarelle*, landscapes, also a few *incisioni*, I like to play with *mitical* subjects, mix up science and ancient history, physics, *chimics*, biology. I like Einstein, Newton, Homer, Petronio – no? – all mixed up together, a kind of *minestra di verdura* . . .'

'Do you sell any of it?'

'Oh, sure, I've exposed a few of my operas – my works, no? – in the *galerie* here, in Venice, Verona, Milano, *in giro*, here and there, wherever. There's a good market, but you have to get inserted in the logic, the *ingranaggio*, know the right people.'

'So who buys your stuff?'

'Everyone. *Contadini*, bank clerks, *poliziotti*, people with restaurants and bars, they love to hang pictures here, embellish their walls, the *salotto*, no? They hang maybe forty, fifty pictures in one room . . .'

Rocco interprets the Pandorese way of life for me. 'All that's required of a woman is to perform well at the table and in bed. *Cucina e famiglia, no?* The men go out to work, bring back the BMW and the fur coat, and *basta*, they're happy as pigs in mud.'

He sees the limitations, but he loves them too. He's entranced by the whole thing, lulled by the language, the beauty, the food, wine, ease, and pleasure of it all. He's beyond recall. Floating in the dark, sweet waters of the womb.

We landed at Gatwick through wind, cloud, and rain, the plane rattling and lurching in over a good fifty miles of congested sky. Good old Britain! The most reliable weather in the world, as I tell my incredulous students. You can rely on it to let you down. Thick sweaters and raincoats are *de rigueur*. In *August*! I ask you.

The streets of London strike me as noisomely filthy and vile, filled with the hopeless and unemployed, dossers wielding beer cans and asking for a sub, shapeless housewives in clashing colours pushing shopping trolleys against the wind, weird Rastafarians wobbling along with their ghetto-blasters and bombed-out eyes . . . And the rich, the cool, sealed-off rich, in their leafy squares, seemingly millions of miles away from the grime that's all around them.

Everyone's obsessed with video and television. No one seems to talk about what they've seen or done in real life; it's all 'Did you see that documentary the other night?' and 'They had a very good programme about that on Channel 4 last week.' Having been away for a bit, I thought things must have improved dramatically since I left. But no, 'the best television in the world' remains as drivelling and smug as ever, with its weathermen like tailors' dummies, news-readers who look as if they have been freshly dug up from the grave, illiterate sports commentators, jackass disc jockeys, elephantine darts champions, melancholy snooker players, po-faced journalists, dreary comedians, and, most grotesque of all, the television personalities — Frost, Wogan, Hunniford, Aspel — even their names sound like something out of a gale warning — endlessly recycled, tattered round the edges, their skin going green from excessive exposure to studio lights — who continue to present and pronounce on every topic imaginable, ranging freely through the field of all human knowledge, science, literature, history, geography, anthropology, breathing banality on it all, withering and shrivelling each subject as they go.

It strikes me that television bears the same relationship to the world as hamburgers do to cows. And people end up thinking television *is* the world — the highest good, the only good, the all-absorbing, the authoritative, the faithful, the timeless, the giver of grace and fountain of youth, bringer of joy and interpreter of disaster, a comfort to the sick, a companion to the old, a guide to the young, an informant to the middle-aged, a weapon to the mighty, a solace to the weak; no ocean is too deep, no desert too vast, no creature nor atom too small, all shall be contained, all accommodated, all recorded with a voice-over, titles, and music, all scheduled and broadcast and repeated, and there shall be follow-up books, and education packs, and viewers' letters, and even the letters shall be broadcast in their turn, and the ratings shall be published, and lo, the dead shall live again, for though their bodies be corrupted their images live on in the archives, and yea, even the unborn shall breathe and gesticulate, and not even the privacy of the womb, nor the hush of the scrotum, no, not the bedrooms of kings and queens shall be sacred, for all shall be penetrated, all made visible, and all shall be video, and all manner of thing shall be video, holy, holy, holy, shalom, shalom, shalom, BBC have mercy on us, ITV have mercy on us, for there is no health in us, we are vile, we are vile, we are vile, brightness falls from the air, Glory, glory, glory, oh lordy lordy, Fast forward, rewind, playback, World without end, Stay tuned, Amen.

If they don't watch out, the British are going to end up the first race on earth with armchair-shaped bodies and scrambled eggs for brains.

I've just had lunch with Sarah. Desolation. I've got no right to be upset, because I've been sleeping around fairly vigorously myself, but I sense Another Person in her life. What's more, I suspect it to be none other than her boss, a millionaire with a lonely heart who's been after her for the past five years. Given Sarah's ambition, her soft spot for bourgeois luxuries, I suppose it's a great credit to her (or possibly me) that she's resisted his gold-plated advances for so long. But now that I'm off the scene she probably figures why the hell not.

She looked older, with a slight shift further towards middle age in her dress, the lines very noticeable round her eyes (the small-print lines, we used to call them), and her skin whiter than I remember. Not a healthy white, either — office-light white. But she's still a good-looking girl, and I can't help thinking what a month in the sun would do to her, on all fronts.

Our conversation was superficial and frustrating. We didn't discuss ourselves, except in the usual cruddy terms of work, flat, films seen, etc. I asked her when she was going to come out and stay. She said she didn't know, she had a lot of work, she'd have to try to find a little gap, perhaps in November . . . In other words she's not interested. Then she asked when I was coming back, and I said not for a good while yet.

'Is Italy that nice?' she asked, and I said, 'Yes, it's great.'

It looks as if our separation has begun in earnest.

Monday 19

Winchester. With Mum and Dad. Scarcely less desolation than with Sarah. Only here it's my sadness for them that grinds into me. What is it exactly? Dad old now, struggling to get about? Mum's excitement at having me home? The huge meals she lays out which I can hardly eat? My old room, with the plastic model battleships in the display cabinet that I've tried so many times to throw away, and never quite managed? My bookshelves with the complete William, Biggles, and Sherlock Holmes? The hideous silver-plated 'thing' – the wrong shape for a plate, too small for a tray, with funny little legs on so you can't really use it for anything – presented to Dad by the Hants District Bus Company for his forty years fixing their engines? The faded grotty print of Van Gogh's 'Sunflowers', framed and glassed on the sitting-room wall? The trains rattling and hooting past as I try to get to sleep? Or is it something intangible – the sense of broken dreams? Their disappointment? The promises of childhood, the Macmillan and Wilson years, all mysteriously gone, slipped like water through the fingers?

I made coffee after supper. Real coffee. Sick of the watery grey washing-machine waste we normally have, I went out and bought a packet of continental dark roast, and made a brew to lift the roof of your mouth off. Mum virtually exploded at the first taste. 'That is far too strong, Paul! You know you shouldn't drink coffee that strong. Doctors say it's very bad for you. It overloads your heart.'

'What do you think, Dad?'

He thought about it. Smacked his lips and licked his yellowy-white moustache. 'It's strong. Your mother's right . . .' He had another sip. 'But it's tasty, all right. Is that how you have it in Italy?'

'More or less.'

Then Mum came swinging irrelevantly in with 'But are you *happy* in Italy?'

'We weren't talking about happiness, Mum, we were talking about coffee.'

'And I want to know if you're happy. What about Sarah?'

'That was coming to an end anyway,' I said.

'Lovely girl,' said Mum. 'I thought you were going to get married . . .'

'All right, I know, only it didn't work out, so you'd better forget her.'

'You gave up all that, your job, your friends, a lovely girl . . .'

'Mum, let me explain very, very carefully. I did not give anything up that wasn't a dead loss anyway. I am now trying something new!'

'Well, how many more new things are you going to try before you settle down and start making use of your education?'

This got me furious. The capacity of parents to think exclusively in clichés. Where did they learn that the phrase 'make use of your education' can only appear in a sentence when accompanied by the verb 'settle down'? And where and when in the history of our race was it decided that settling down was such a big deal in the first place?

I tried to explain. 'I am making use of my education precisely *not* to settle down. I'm using it to live abroad, and I'm very grateful for my education, and to you and Dad for all the sacrifices you made so that I could get it, because it's given me the freedom to get away from what I regard as a very sick country with a barbaric government and find out what living really is.'

This silenced her, but she was not convinced. She got up, walked silently into the kitchen, and poured her cup of coffee down the sink.

Dad looked pained.

'Look, Dad,' I said, 'if you want to try that coffee the real Italian way, put a drop of this stuff in it.' And I showed him the bottle of grappa I'd brought over.

'Go on, then, just a drop.'

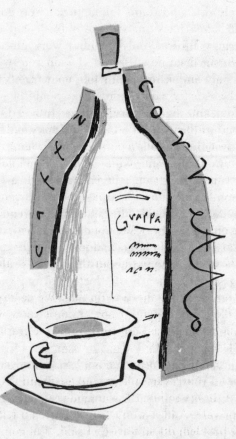

'They call this *caffè corretto.*' I sloshed a good measure into his cup. 'That'll warm you up. You'll feel like a young lad again.'

He took a sip and spluttered; then another, and laughed.

'What do you think?'

'I think they're on to something with this,' he said. 'That'll put hairs on your chest, all right . . . It's bloody good, eh?'

Mum came back in, stirring a fresh cup of sugary mouse-grey effluent.

When she'd sat down, I said, 'I want you two to come out to Italy and see what it's like for yourselves.'

I knew exactly what the reaction would be – a sort of uncomfortable shifting in their chairs, as if their backsides had suddenly been attacked by ants, and a hunt for the perfect excuse while a parade of really lame ones came dribbling out in a feeble whine: 'Oh, I don't know, there's all the fuss of getting there, and getting back, the suitcases, I don't know if my passport's still valid . . . and there's the cat to look after, the milk to cancel, we're getting on, you know, we're not as young as we used to be, travelling's for the young, and all these terrorists at the airports, and then what about the cost of it all . . .?'

'I'll pay.'

'Oh no, there's no need to do that. We've got a bit put away. If we don't spend it now, I don't know what we'll spend it on.' This was Dad, or possibly the grappa getting to work inside him.

'Oh, Arthur, you never know. You just never know. If that hip of yours starts playing up again, and you have to go in for the operation, the way things are now you'll have to go private. And it won't be cheap, I can tell you.'

'The problem doesn't arise,' I said. 'I'm going to book you on a flight out, and I'm going to pay. Just give me a date.'

Mum started shifting in her seat again, but the perfect excuse was eluding her. A few years ago she'd have crushed the idea with a swift snap of her jaws. Now she just sat there looking hopeless.

'Well, do you want to go or not?' I asked.

'I don't think so, dear,' said Mum, and Dad said, 'Let's think about it.'

'No, don't think about it. Decide. I'd like to do this for you. Please don't let me down. Just think. Italy! You've never been there. Venice, Florence, the Alps . . .'

'I'm not going up any mountains,' said Mum.

'All right, no mountains. Will you come?'

'Give us a chance to think. We'll discuss it in bed tonight. I'll do my best to persuade her.'

And then Mum noticed it was five past nine and time to switch on the news.

Mum and Dad finally decided that perhaps they'd better not come to Italy after all. Not this year anyway. I said nothing, because I think if they want to be boring, that's their business.

A couple of days later I decided I'd had enough and took the plane back to Pandoro.

On the plane I met a girl called Giulia.

She was sitting in the window seat, looking pale. I was struck by her pallor, because it was set off so violently by her cascading black hair. Her face was fine-featured and intelligent.

I sat down next to her, and, taking a stab at the cause of her bloodless state, said, 'Don't worry, statistics prove that more people are killed every year playing billiards than in planes.'

She was surprised. 'How do you know I'm afraid?'

'You look it. Anyway, most people are.'

'I know it's safe,' she said, 'statistically, theoretically, mechanically . . . But it doesn't *feel* safe. That's the problem.'

Once the plane was up in the sky, we got talking. She'd been to London to buy books and practise her English. She's studying medicine. I at once had the feeling of a terribly serious person, so serious she was almost afraid to laugh. She was also, judging by her clothes and jewellery, rather rich. She showed no special interest in me.

I immediately took her as a challenge. It became vital to me to engage her in conversation, show sympathy, tact, brilliance, get her talking, get her interested, get her phone number. But like a poor-quality mesmerist, I suspect I succeeded only in hypnotizing myself, while she sat there, clear-eyed and cool, looking detached and faintly impatient.

We landed in Pandoro. The passengers clapped on touchdown. Giulia was met by a burly rustic type in a check shirt and straw hat, who carried her bags to a lustrous grey Mercedes. She offered me a lift into town.

'Great,' I said, 'thanks', and on the way there I scribbled my phone number on a piece of paper and gave it to her.

'What am I going to do with that?' she asked.

'Use it in an emergency.'

She smiled. 'What sort of emergency?'

'I don't know. That's up to you. You might be robbed, or attacked, or . . . stuck for a word in English. Or you may just feel like meeting for coffee one rainy morning.'

'Well,' she said, 'let's see', and she put the slip of paper in her handbag and observed how nice it was to be back in the hot weather again.

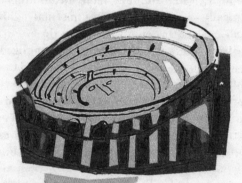

There isn't much going on in Pandoro, and I'm wondering whether I shouldn't have stuck it out in Britain a bit longer. Gone off to the Edinburgh Festival or something. I'm really just hanging around here. Of course, idleness breeds introspection, and introspection breeds melancholy, and the only solution to that is soaking up industrial quantities of beer in the Piazza della Signoria — which is scarcely a solution at all, because even that gets depressing if you do it for too long.

I brought my guitar and amp back from England — last night I dusted it down, tuned it up, and had a little twangle. To beguile the weary hours. Only it didn't work. I notice a strange emptiness inside me, as if I'm waiting for something to happen.

Today, for a change of air, I took a bus out to the lake. The cult spot on this side is Punta San Petronio, with a little harbour and hotel, about which Laurence Olivier and Vivien Leigh are said to have flitted amorously in youthful days — presumably before they started throwing china at each other. Behind the hotel there's a Renaissance villa, protected by thick walls and iron gates. You never see anyone there. It's said to be inhabited by a single miserable old lady who spends all day wrapped up in a blanket, being wheeled from room to room by a muscular German nurse.

North of the villa lies Baia delle Sirene, Mermaid Bay, where groves of olive and cypress slope gently down to the shore — or so the guidebook says. I've never experienced it myself, since you have to pay twelve thousand lire to get in. Proles like me crawl through a fence a few hundred yards up and swim from some rubbish-strewn rocks where guidebook writers never tread.

I bumped into Rocco there, and he invited me for a voyeuristic paddle in his inflatable dinghy.

'Voyeuristic?'

'Yeah. We'll go and see the *integrali*, no? The wholefood-munchers, bare-assed astrology freaks, naturists, fennels –'

'Fennels?'

'Yeah, *finocchi*, no?'

'Oh. Gays.'

'Yeah. Only place they can come out in the open and bronze their *atrezzi*. You can bet they're all good momma's boys when they get home, though. Jeez, look at that one . . .'

He nodded towards a lone plump figure on a rock at the end of the beach. Nude but for a floppy sunhat, he sat engrossed in a book, his legs spread wide apart, providing a vista of pink and hairless genitals beneath a rotund paunch. It was one of those images that you know you will never forget, however hard you try – gross, repulsive, and unsettling, yet somehow aesthetically complete.

The man had courage, though, there's no denying that. Unappetizing sight that he was, he must, I suppose, have been sustained by the belief (or perhaps it's a statistical certainty) that he is beautiful to someone. He was doing his best to find that someone. I can only wish him luck.

Listless, hazy weather. Spent the day at the pool, reading *Great Expectations*, which I'm supposed to be teaching next year.

There's a noticeable lack of decent bodies around. A lot of loose flesh. Wobbling cellulite. Fallen angels. Perhaps all the beauties are away at the coast. Or perhaps the Italians simply look better in clothes.

Tuesday 27

I realized this morning what it is I've been waiting for. I met her in the street, shopping with her mother. They looked like a pair of models from *Vogue*.

I came up alongside them outside Gianfranco Ferré. 'Giulia!'

Her mother nearly fell off her high heels. 'Who is this person?' she asked with a basilisk look in her eye.

'An Englishman I met on the plane from London.'
'Ah.'

I offered her my hand. 'Paul,' I said.

She took it with a small show of reluctance. 'Grimani,' she muttered.

I suggested coffee. They declined.

'Giulia,' I said, 'don't forget to call me.'

She smiled, as one smiles at a child, and they set off again, arm in arm.

I went into a bar and checked the name in the telephone directory. Five Grimanis were listed. I got some *gettoni* and started dialling. Struck gold with my second call. 'Signorina Giulia is out with her mother. Please try again at lunchtime.' So there it is. The address is 1 Piazza della Signoria. About as chic as you can get. I'll bet they own the whole square.

Thursday
29

Persuaded Giulia to meet me for tea in the square beneath (or is it in?) her house. We got off to a pretty poor start. She seemed determined not to enjoy herself; spent the first ten minutes either wincing or looking as if she was about to.

I asked her if she liked music.

'Of course I like music. What a question!'

'What kind?'

'Mozart, Bach, Ockeghem . . .'

'Who?'

'Never mind.'

'Do you go to a lot of concerts?'

A tired look. 'We have a box at La Scala.'

'Oh.'

'And at La Fenice. But we don't use that much.'

'No, quite. One doesn't, I suppose . . . Now what about jazz? Do you like that at all?'

'I don't understand it.'

'You don't need to understand it! You just go with it. Like sex.'

She looked doubtful. 'Nobody has ever explained it to me.'

'What? Sex?'

A wince, then – very icily – 'Jazz.'

'Not that it makes any difference,' I went on, 'because jazz is essentially sex translated into music, as I think you'll agree when you hear my Ben Webster tapes. Do you know Ben Webster?'

'No.'

'Well, you've got to hear him. You've absolutely got to. Then you'll know what I'm talking about. People die miserably every day for the lack of music like that.'

Her eyebrows arched exquisitely. 'Oh yes?'

'Oh yes. No one's experience is complete without it.'

'No one's experience is ever complete.'

'Yeah, OK, OK. *Touché.*'

I offered to drop the tapes round later on, but she said she was going to Asolo.

'Who – or what – is Asolo?' I asked.

'Oh,' she said. 'I thought all Englishmen knew about Asolo.'

'Not this one. What's so special about it?'

'Browning lived there.'

'He lived in lots of places. His wife even lived in Wimpole Street, as I recall, but it remains somewhat drab.'

'Asolo's delightful.'

'Well, if you're short of a companion . . .'

She gave me a cool look. 'I'm going to see my grandmother. She's an invalid. I will spend three days with her, and then come home. It will not be very exciting. She has no other company.'

'Perhaps I could come and play her my Ben Webster tapes?'

Giulia laughed. The first time! It was glorious – a sudden freeing of restraining forces – like a river unfrozen in spring.

'You are so beautiful when you laugh,' I said.

She immediately stopped. 'Don't say that.'

'It's true.'

'Don't, all the same. I must go now. Thank you for the tea.'

'Call me when you get back.'

'I'll try to remember,' she said, rising, and walked away.

| **Saturday 31** | By arrangement with Rocco, Bill, Mike, and a few others, we held an informal kick-around in preparation for the new football season. Or rather we intended to, but found the ground occupied by a match. It was part of a tournament organized by a certain 'Archie'. |

'Who's Archie?' I asked.

'Not Archie. ARCI.'

'What's that?'

'Leisure and sporting arm of the Communist Party.'

'You mean these guys are all Communists?'

'No. Anyone can join ARCI.'

'Why don't we?'

'Nothing to stop us,' said Bill.

'What do you think, Rocco?'

'I don't know. I need to check my *agenda*. I'm going to be *in giro* a lot this fall. Don't want to tie myself down . . .'

'Mike?'

'Yeah, OK. As long as it doesn't cost too much.'

So we asked about joining the league, but no one there had the faintest idea how to go about it. The teams had mysterious 'presidents' who did all the organization and didn't come to their games. The best lead we could get was the name of a guy called Gigi, who has a bar in the Industrial Zone and seems to constitute the spiritual centre of Communist football in Pandoro.

So we got into Bill's car and voyaged south into the commercial heartland of Pandoro: miles of warehouses, lorry parks, and concrete fencing. After much wandering, we found Gigi's bar. The Bar Sport.

Gigi was one of those big, blond, meaty physiques – complete with stubble, tattooed forearms, and fifty-litre stomach – that take you so much by surprise in a country like Italy. He looked like a classic son of Hamburg, Huddersfield, or Detroit.

We ordered beer and told him our problem.

'There are two possibilities,' he said. 'Either you join ARCI or an unofficial league.'

'Which do you suggest?'

'It's up to you. I'm organizing a tournament next month. Registration closes tomorrow evening.'

'How do we register?'

'You nominate fifteen players and a manager. You pay a deposit of one hundred and fifty thousand lire to cover fines for bad language and fouls. There are four groups. Each group plays four matches, and the top two from each group go through to the quarter-finals, the semi-finals, and so on. There's a third-place play-off, and the first three teams get cups. Are you insured?'

Mike, Bill, and I looked at each other. 'Insured?'

'Yes. Your team must be insured for injuries caused to others or their property.'

'No, we're not.'

'What about medical certificates? Got those?'

'Erm, no.'

'A president, secretary, treasurer, two auditors, and two *probiviri*?'

'What the hell are *probiviri*?'

'Guarantors.'

'Are they necessary?'

'Oh yes.'

'Well, we haven't got them.'

Gigi looked bilious. 'What the hell have you got?'

'We've got a team,' said Mike. 'Just.'

'Forget it,' said Gigi. 'You've got to be properly organized.'

'Can't we just get together with other teams for a simple game of football?'

'There's no such thing as a simple game of football.'

'What about joining ARCI? Is that any easier?'

'Joining's easy. It's playing that's difficult.'

'What do you mean?'

'The organizer's a *deficiente*. He books matches without a pitch to play on, or he tells the teams two different dates. Or the same date but different times. Or the same date, the same time, but two different pitches. He gets every combination but the right one. If you enjoy that kind of *casino*, join by all means.'

We thanked him for his help, ordered another round of beer, and quietly dropped the subject.

I'm annoyed about the football.

I think I need it – or something like it – to drive away the blues, which are increasingly, insidiously present in my life. Why, I don't know. Sometimes I think it's the sheer ease of Italian living – the fact that I don't need to work more than four or five hours a day to make a decent income, thus eliminating the struggle for daily bread which is such a key element of life in puritan lands. Or I may be missing the edge on things that you only get from living in your own language – where odd words, nuances, metaphors, innuendoes, looks, pauses, inflections can make the simplest conversation amusing, or threatening, or somehow bigger than its explicit content.

Or maybe – a related thought – foreigners don't pick up the elements of struggle in the natives' existence, whether through diplomacy or insensitivity, and so come to find it all bland and over-smooth. Maybe I miss the dinginess of Britain – because when you have it around you, it makes you feel clever to rise above it. Maybe that's what makes life worth living after all – staying ahead of the game, keeping your nostrils above the sewage. Only the paradox is, it seems you *need* the sewage.

Maybe I just miss Sarah. Or Giulia. Or Jane. Or just being with a woman.

Monday 9

My cousin Colin has rolled up from London to stay a couple of weeks. He's not my favourite person in the universe – a self-centred, depressive art student with a droning voice and questionable personal hygiene – but at least he should take my mind off the destructive and melancholy topic of myself.

He's come to Italy on the instruction of his tutor, who sounds like an unusually enlightened person. She told him he had no hope of becoming an artist if the only pictures he ever looked at were album covers. Hear, hear. What a marvellous, old-style teacherly thing to say. Unashamed use of maturer perspectives and experience. Well done, old girl. I'm surprised people like that are allowed to exist in art colleges any more.

So he's got to go to the Uffizi in Florence, the Brera in Milan, and the Accademia in Venice, and write some kind of report. She even managed to wangle him a grant for it.

I asked him if he liked – or knew anything about – Italian painting.

'No,' he said. 'But I hear the wine's cheap.'

I had an invitation from some Italian footballing friends to a 'pyjama party' this weekend at Lido degli Estensi, down on the coast near Ferrara. I thought the experience might be an eye-opener for Colin, and accepted.

Lido degli Estensi is a classic holiday ghetto. Vast, umbrella-crammed beach, hotels, trashy shops, amusement arcades, the lot. But the light redeems it. Light that photographers dream of: hot, clear, and brilliant, sculpting all it falls on, turning even the rubbish to gold.

We went for a swim in the resplendent afternoon. The sea looked most inviting from a distance, but turned out to be a murky turd-green in colour when you got closer, with an oily, sick sheen to its surface. I took a deep breath and plunged in, sported manfully awhile, and emerged with my skin itching fearsomely. I rushed to the showers to wash off the various domestic and industrial effluents that coated my epidermis before they could do too much damage. I shudder to think what they would do if they got into your blood, through a cut or something.

I worried, briefly, about Colin, because his death-pale skin is full of eruptions, blotches, slashes, crusts, pimples, sores, discolorations, and vile tetters of the most diverse kinds, which would presumably make a royal highway for the entry of contagion; but then I thought, no, the pollutants are more likely to catch something horrific off him.

He looked skeletal and diseased next to the trim, sunburnt, muscular bodies of our hosts – what an image of British youth! He tried on an expression of silent, glowering intensity whenever he was spoken to, but the Italians quickly and expertly cut through that and soon had him chatting happily in the manner of a normal, well-balanced human being.

One of the group, a certain Marco, had a birthday. They made him close his eyes for his present, and sang '*Tanti auguri a te*' while he stood there giggling, waiting for the worst. It soon came. On the final resounding note of the song someone snatched down his swimsuit from behind, and a platter of whipped cream was flung at his midriff, exploding magnificently over his tackle, which suddenly appeared sculpted in white foam. When he tried to pull up his swimsuit again, there were raucous objections. 'Let the girls lick it off!' 'Don't spoil their fun!' 'What about the poofs?' 'Let's see if Claudia can do it with her tongue without giving him an erection!'

Claudia was Marco's girlfriend and willingly obliged.

A commentary – ball by ball, one might say – was provided by a lawyer called Enzo. 'She's licking around the root of the organ now, and yes! I think I saw a sign of excitement there! It's stirring . . . it's stirring . . . it's definitely moving! Can he hold it down? Think of other things, Marco, your work, think of the Italian economy, that never goes up . . . But no, she's too strong for him, look at that speed as she goes up the shaft! Don't get indigestion, Claudia! . . . It's rising! It's rising! . . . It's up! Ladies and gentlemen, it is up! . . . Well, well, what a performance! What a victory! She played him like a violin! What a prodigy! A phenomenon! A veritable Juventus!'

After the beach festivities, supper in a local trattoria, and all back to the apartment to put on our pyjamas. There were silk pyjamas, satin pyjamas, stripy cotton pyjamas, leopard-skin winceyette pyjamas, pyjamas in track-suit style and boiler-suit style, pyjamas that looked like surplus stock from the psychiatric service, others that seemed salvaged from first-class cabins on the *Titanic*. There were nightshirts, body-stockings, kimonos, and one brave or forgetful fellow with stripes painted directly on his body. The odd thing was, though, that once the initial joke had worn off, it became rather dull. There wasn't anything to talk about, since we'd all been together since the afternoon, and as usual nobody was seriously interested in getting drunk. A pair of party-sevens stood largely untapped, except by Colin and me, while everyone else drank Fanta. *Fanta!* I couldn't believe my eyes.

There was one memorable moment when a couple of six-foot volley-ball players announced, '*Palle fuori!*' and by some sleight of hand managed to hide their penises inside their pyjamas while hanging their balls out through the slit in front. And what wondrous balls! The size of eggs, and bristling black. The fashion quickly spread, and soon all the gentlemen present were displaying their merchandise in a similar way.

'What do you think?' I asked Colin.

'Weird,' he said. 'Totally weird.' And then one of the volley-ball players shouted, '*Palle dentro!*' and everyone put their balls away.

The party dragged on till two o'clock or thereabouts, when everyone crashed out wherever they could find a space. It was extremely cramped . . . twelve people to a room, on the floor, in chairs, the lucky few in bed . . . and very hard to sleep.

At seven I got up and walked out along the sea front to get a coffee. The place looked terrific empty, and I read the paper in a café, with brioche and cappuccino, surveying the deserted beach with a curious and powerful feeling of exhilaration.

Thursday 12	Colin's away in Milan today. Mercifully. I'm coming to find him deeply disgusting. Apart from the usual problems with 'arty' guests – who don't wash up, don't cook, don't buy food, and are fantastically slow on the draw when it comes to paying for drinks – he has the incredible knack of predicting exactly when I'm about to need the toilet and darting in there a split second before me. This is somehow more enervating than all his other vices put together.

A parallel knack is that of being silent when I most feel like talking, and talking when I most feel like being silent. This is his perversity, not mine, incidentally – he won't talk at table, or over a glass of wine, but suddenly opens up when I'm settling into a book or some work and my entire body language expresses the concept Do Not Disturb. I've been trying unsuccessfully for the past four days to finish *Great Expectations*, but Colin won't let me.

Another thing is his eating habits. Bent low over his plate, breathing heavily, he forks the food impatiently through pendent unshaven lips and chews noisily with his mouth open, like a moron with a blocked nose. When he's finished, he licks his fingers and wipes them on his trousers. The whole performance is so repulsive that I've taken to avoiding meals at home, or, when that's not possible, bringing a book to the table. Next it'll be earplugs and dark glasses.

As far as I can gather from our rather unsatisfactory conversations, he's not a happy person. He seems to expect failure in everything he undertakes. I even had to force him to go to Milan. He kept saying it would be too difficult, too much 'sweat', and when I pointed out that he was obliged by the terms of his grant to go, he shrugged his shoulders and said, 'They've already paid.'

I had hoped Italy would do more for him. Open him out. Put a little sunshine in his gloomy Nordic soul. It's supposed to, dammit. But after the brief promise of the pyjama party, he seems to have retreated into an armour of deadness to the outside world. I suppose there is a limit to what even Italy can do with someone who walks around her medieval streets listening to Heavy Metal on a Walkman.

Should I try harder to talk to him? Offer some interest in his work, his hobbies? Does he have hobbies? Does he do any work, for that matter? I haven't seen him draw a single line. He gives so little away. Just this permanent surly look that says, 'Leave me alone. I'm a dead loss, and I like it that way.' But something in me, an unconscious missionary urge, or my new-found interest in teaching, tells me to try to penetrate that, hack a path through the obstreperous undergrowth of crassness and egotism, help to free the strangled life that's inside him — must be inside him, because it's in all of us if we can only find it. And then I think, leave it out, Paul, you sound like a parent; you're getting old and stupid. You don't 'save' people — they save themselves or die.

Friday 13

Over breakfast – trying to keep my eyes off Colin slurping at his plate – I asked about the trip to Milan.

'Got busted on the train.'

'Oh no, Colin! What for?'

'Hadn't got a ticket.'

'Why not?'

'Didn't want to buy one.'

Something snapped inside me. I was suddenly fed up with his endless ungrateful parasitism. I told him he was a fool. If there's one place where you shouldn't try to cheat the railways – because you don't need to – it's Italy.

'It was four quid to Milan,' he said.

'Four quid? That's peanuts! It's 150 miles away. D'you know how far you'd get in Britain on four quid? Twenty miles – if you were lucky.'

'It's all money.'

'Of course it is! What the hell do you expect? Free travel for social deviants?'

Colin heaved in a mouthful of bread and jam and muttered through it, 'Yeah, well, I don't believe in the monetary system.'

'Very convenient,' I said. 'And what would you put in its place? A barter economy? Beads? Or just free everything?'

He shrugged. 'Maybe.'

'Let's face it, Colin,' I said, 'you don't believe in anything, do you?'

He stared into his coffee-cup, his face a mask of indifference. Then, without bothering to answer my question, he shuffled off to the bathroom, whence his usual *aubade* of grunts, sighs, trickles, groans, hisses, farts, splashes, etc. drove me hurriedly out to complete my breakfast in a bar.

I desperately need a break from this barbarian. He disgusts me at all levels. Somehow I've got to put up with another eight days of him.

| **Saturday 14** | Figuring Giulia must be back from Asolo by now, I phoned her home. But, alas, no cigar — she's gone to Siena. I wonder who she's seeing this time. She'll be back tomorrow evening, they say. I really feel like seeing her. Her freshness and clarity. A necessary antidote to Colin. |

Forced Colin to go to Florence, and so managed at last to finish *Great Expectations*. The lack of C's intrusive presence in the house wonderfully balmy and soothing.

No luck with Giulia yet, but elsewhere life is picking up: the scattered community is beginning to reassemble — after something like ten weeks off for the summer.

Had a meeting at the university — to discuss exams and next year's courses. The usual chaos, the usual barefaced attempts to avoid work or even the thought of work. Yet again there is no co-ordination of the exams, so the Second Year papers will be more difficult than the Third Year, the Fourth Year will probably be the easiest of the lot, and the poor First Years will be required to decode utterances that would bamboozle the compilers of the *Oxford English Dictionary*. As usual I complain, and as usual there's an awkward silence, and then someone says, 'I suppose we could show each other the papers we set', and I say, 'Fine. When?' and there's another silence. Eventually Ferruzzi wades in with a tirade about 'self-disciplined autonomy' and draws a threefold parallel with the Co-operative Movement, Sir Edmund Hillary's assault on Everest, and *The Taming of the Shrew*, the point of which not even he appears to see.

He then looks at his watch and says, 'Well, gentlemen, is there anything else? Because I've got to pick up my wife from the station at 3.30 . . . No? Good. I will leave you to sort it out, as I'm sure you can, being young and able-bodied.'

His sidekick, Professor Calpestrelli, a big tough Marxist with an encyclopedic knowledge of the railway timetable, announces, 'I have to be in Milan by five. I can make the 3.32 if you give me a lift now.' And off they go, another set of responsibilities successfully dodged.

The meeting dribbles to a close. We have failed to decide anything useful, and the courses for the coming year, starting in just six weeks' time, are still only very vaguely defined. But nobody gives a damn. It's great to work in a university — you can be as lazy, uncaring, and irresponsible as you like – and there's no one to call you to book.

Came home to find Colin slumped in the same armchair, in the same position as he'd been in when I set out two hours previously, reading a copy of *Rolling Stone* that he'd brought over with him. What a depressing guy.

Rang Giulia to invite her out for a pizza, but she was busy. Why, I ask myself, do I bother – with anything?

What A Day. What A Stinker of A Day. Went down to the **Wednesday**
university library to get some background literature on **18**
Dickens, and found it was shut because of staff shortages.
Then, rather than go home and face Colin, I took a stroll
through town, thinking vaguely of buying some new
trousers. At the bottom of Via Cavour I saw a large group
of people gathered round a car. I thought at first there'd
been an accident, but it turned out to be a Ferrari, which
they were all busy admiring. *'Che bella macchina!'* *È*
stupenda!' *'Una meraviglia!'* They appreciated the white
leather seats, the gear-stick, the steering wheel, the sweep
of the body, even the exhaust pipe, which was very fat and
rimmed with chrome. Then there was a flurry of
excitement as someone noticed the fog-lamps attached to
the front bumper. Apparently these were of the type that
mere mortals attach to their front bumpers. A great sigh of
indignation went up. *'Oh, ma guarda che schifo!'* How
disgusting, how incredibly tasteless! They were really
shocked. A person who could afford a hundred and fifty
million lire for a Ferrari, and goes and puts *ordinary*
fog-lamps on the front. What a vandal! What a cheap-
skate! What a crumb!

Suddenly everyone was silent. The 'crumb' had
appeared. People who had only moments ago been
denouncing him as a delinquent and a philistine now
backed away in awe. He opened the door – which was
unlocked – and climbed in. He was blond, with rather
blunt features, not more than twenty-five, and wore a
loud but beautifully cut cotton shirt and navy-blue
trousers. He started the engine. A *frisson* stole through the
spectators at its grating roar. The Ferrari crawled forward
a few feet, then came to a stop again outside a
pastry-shop. A girl came out of the shop, holding a parcel
and laughing. Someone next to me said, *'Che bella!'* and I
said, *'Sì'* as she extended one exquisitely white-stockinged

leg into the car, then swung down into the passenger seat, and gave the driver a kiss. They were like Hollywood lovers. The Ferrari roared again and sped off among more appreciative sighs, and I only half-registered its Siena number-plate, because my mind was obsessed by the fact that the girl in the crumb's Ferrari, her head resting on his shoulder, was – of course, because I'm having a sod's luck these days – the elusive, the delectable, the very cold – Giulia.

I suppose I realized then that she was totally out of my league. I also suppose this depressed me. There was no time to notice, however, because the next thing I knew, Aldo – my policeman student from the Buckingham School – spotted me and hurried over.

'Paul,' he said, 'we need you. There's a madman – English or Irish or American, I don't know – standing on the top of the amphitheatre and he says he's going to throw himself off. We need someone to speak to him.'

'What about you, Aldo? Your English is very good.'

'No,' Aldo sighed. 'I can't say, "How are you?" and "Do you like fish and chips?" in this situation.'

'Sounds good enough to me.'

Aldo laughed, but tensely. 'Come on, we must be quick.'

I followed him to the Roman amphitheatre, a vast ring of brick and marble that sits in the centre of town like a crashed spacecraft from an unknown civilization. Aldo hurried me in through the cordon of police, and we ran up the dark stairways to the top. I stepped out on to the parapet, and there, six feet away, on an uneven piece of wall, trembling like a nervous swimmer, stood Colin.

'Oh bloody hell, what is this, Colin? What are you doing?'

'I'm going to jump off.'

'Don't do that, Colin. Please.'

'I'm going to.'

'Don't. It's pointless.'

'It's pointless going on.'

'Things will change.' I felt very little conviction saying this. 'They'll get better. It's awful being a student, I know. But things improve. You've got your whole life in front of you!'

'No. It's all behind me now.'

'Don't talk like that, Colin. That's defeatism, giving in to the rubbish of life, the death forces. You've got to realize this is just a mood. You'll get over it, like any other mood.'

'It is NOT a mood! It's been going on for five years now.'

'What about your art? Doesn't that mean anything to you?'

'That's all a big wanker's game. I've had enough.'

'It's no solution, though, is it? Killing yourself?'

'Course it's a solution! Put an end to all the crap.'

'Look, Colin,' I said, expressing the first thought that came into my head, 'how do you know that when you die there isn't a part of you that lives on?'

'I don't believe in all that Christian rubbish. You just go out and that's it. It's all over.'

'But you don't know that!'

'Sod off. What do you care?'

'I care very much.'

'Yeah? Well, I've read your diary. I know what you think of me. You think I'm a prat.'

'I don't!'

'You do. You think I'm disgusting.'

'You really read my diary?'

'Yeah.'

'That's a shameful thing to do. You *are* a prat.'

'Yeah, well, we've got that straight now, so don't tell me you care, OK?'

'All right, damn you! I don't care. I think you're a wanker of the first order. A mega-wanker. Does that make you feel any better?'

'Least you're being honest. Now, if you don't mind, I'd like to kill myself, so could you please piss off?'

'Gladly,' I said, and turned away.

I turned back. 'Look, Colin,' I said, 'this is totally ridiculous. You can't kill yourself on a day like this! The sun shining, the city laid out beneath you, with those wonderful terracotta-tile roofs. Why don't we just go and have a drink in the square down there? That café over there, the Petrarca. Can you see it? They do a terrific aperitif. Then we can have a pizza, maybe go out to the lake for a swim. How about it?'

He hesitated. 'No,' he said finally. 'I'm going to jump.'

'The thing is,' I said quickly, trying to get the thought in before he could move, 'if you're going to fail in life, you should at least do it with some style.'

'I don't give a toss about style any more.'

'Clearly. That's just your problem. You haven't lived enough. You're stuck inside that poisonous cliché of punk. You've swallowed all the crap you've been fed, and now, it seems to me, only now, out on top of this wall, you're starting to realize what it is to be an individual, a real person, someone who decides for himself, and not one of a great moronic identically dressed crowd, baying for records and drugs and hate . . .'

Before I could finish, he stepped over the edge.

I felt ill. Aldo came up behind me, and gently took my arm.

'How the hell could he do that?' I said. 'How the hell could he do it?'

'These marginals are impossible,' said Aldo. 'They use drugs, they go crazy . . . they want to destroy themselves. In the end it's their problem.'

'He was my cousin.'

'*Madonna!* No!'

'Yes.'

'You should have told me. I'm sorry, Paul. Really sorry.'

'It's OK. I agree with you anyway. He wants to destroy himself, it's his problem.'

Aldo shook his head. 'When it's in the family, it's your problem too.'

In the street we found a crowd of chattering people, with police and firemen struggling this way and that among them. An ambulance was parked close by.

'Let us in,' cried Aldo.

'Let us out,' cried the officials.

The crowd eventually parted, and two ambulance men emerged, carrying a stretcher. I caught a glimpse of a pale, very calm face above a red blanket.

With Aldo's help I got into the ambulance, and we went tearing through the suburbs till we reached the hospital. The ambulance men cut a swath through the waiting casualty patients, barged through a pair of thick translucent plastic doors, and laid the stretcher down before a large, bored-looking doctor.

'What happened?'

'He fell off the amphitheatre.'

'Jumped,' said the other.

'Where did he land?'

'The firemen caught him in their jump-sheet. They say he banged his head.'

Still bored, the doctor felt Colin's wrist, then examined his head, separating the matted, yellow, gel-stiffened spikes of his hair with obvious distaste.

'Take him to Neurology,' he said, and walked away.

I waited in the Neurology corridor for at least an hour. Eventually a doctor came out and said, 'The X-rays show a small fracture in the rear part of the skull. He's concussed, but not severely.'

'You mean he'll survive?'

The doctor looked slightly puzzled. 'Of course he'll survive. There's no question about that.'

'Do many people survive jumping off the amphitheatre?'

'Your friend jumped off the amphitheatre?'

'Yes.'

He shook his head. 'I understood that he fell over while he was walking.'

'It was a pretty special fall.'

He frowned. 'That means there's a psychiatric dimen-
sion.'

'You bet,' I said.

I left the hospital, had lunch, and went back at five. Colin
was awake. He seemed very calm.

'Well,' I said, 'you made it.'

'Yeah.'

'Are you glad?'

'Dunno.'

'You're lucky the firemen caught you.'

He nodded. 'How long have I got to stay?'

'The doctor said ten days at least. For observation and tests.'

'I'll miss my plane.'

'Yes.' I shuddered at the thought.

He looked out of the window. 'I'm supposed to get to Venice,' he said.

'Don't worry about that. First get better. You've got a fractured skull, you know.'

'Fractured brain too.'

'No,' I said. 'You're a bit mixed up, that's all.'

'Huh!' He gave a harsh laugh. 'A bit!'

He was silent for a few moments. I looked at the floor, wondering what to say.

When I looked up again, his eyes were full of tears. I suddenly saw not Colin, the repellent art student, but a confused and terrified boy.

'Colin,' I said, 'don't worry. Everything's OK now.'

'It's not,' he said, the tears spilling out on to his cheeks. 'Nothing's OK. Nothing at all is OK. I even failed to kill myself.'

'I don't believe this! You've had the luck of the devil. You've had the luxury of committing suicide without actually dying, you've been plucked from the jaws of death by a miracle. If ever there was a person singled out by fate for a charmed life, it's you! You should be grateful for it. The doctor said you've got a skull that's built like the foothills of the Alps – now use it to make something of your life!'

He seemed frightened by what I was saying.

'OK, OK, Colin.' I took his hand. 'I'll stop lecturing you. That's the last thing you need.'

'No one wants to know,' said Colin, now sobbing aloud. 'They never have.'

And who can blame them, I thought.

I staggered out of the hospital at nine o'clock, by which time we had been through the whole catastrophe of his life: his schooldays — cut short by a drugs bust; fights with his parents; leaving home; squatting in Camberwell; drugs again; art college; more drugs; yearnings to be a pop star . . . It was a squalid, unguided mess. No one had talked to him seriously about any of this since he left school at sixteen, and probably not even before then. Now he's twenty-three, and all washed up — or so he thinks. (God, to be twenty-three again!)

The poor fellow needs help. There's no question about it. But where is he going to find it?

Saturday 21

To add to the general gloom, Italo Calvino has just died. The newspapers have gone bananas. He was one of the country's big exports – like Fellini, Armani, Ferrari – one of those exceptional beings who, having risen above the general mediocrity of their homeland, turn out to be far above even the best of other countries too. He seemed a charmed character, one of the gods. People like that aren't supposed to *die*!

They broadcast an old interview with him on TV this evening. Asked by the interviewer to produce 'three keys or talismans for the year 2000', he said we should learn poetry by heart, do complex mathematical calculations by hand, and live in the knowledge that all we have can be taken from us at any time. A lovely, smiling man – and, like so many intellectuals, he would like nothing better than to turn back the clock of history.

The longer I stay in Italy, the more mixed up I feel about it. It can produce a genius like Calvino, and yet the place is generally a most egregious mess. (A lot of people find this congenial, of course, because it answers a mess in themselves. They feel that if a country can be so shambolic and yet trundle along quite comfortably, then why not a person.) Something in this bizarre land gets lost between the individual and the community, so that the whole adds up mysteriously to a great deal less than the sum of its parts.

Perhaps, as Calvino said, they need more calculations done by hand.

I presume Calvino didn't want to die. Meanwhile Colin, who did, is looking better every day. I've been out to the hospital most afternoons and what with his being pinned down there, no longer chomping my food and occupying my toilet, I find him much less threatening.

We've talked some more about his life, and particularly his future. Beyond the mere doggedness of finishing his art course, he seems to have no plans. I can't fathom whether 'art' means anything to him or if he really thinks it's just a 'wanker's game'. When I ask him about it, his brain seems to shudder to a halt (not that it was exactly buzzing along before).

Monday
23

University exams started today. Up at eight, cappuccino and brioche in town, back to work with energy, freshness, and a Positive Mental Attitude.

Well, why not? It may be unlike me, but without change we die.

Harold Ure and I amused ourselves by awarding the Lay of the Year Prize as we sat invigilating. This was followed by the Worst Lay of the Year, and the Worst Male Lay. We got into hysterical laughter when Harold gave the Worst Male Lay to a nun, and had to take a sobering walk outside.

After the morning session we had a long and boozy lunch at the Cacciatore, a good, cheap, off-the-cuff family trattoria. In that convivial atmosphere I found my colleagues surprisingly human and pleasant. Started to feel that if I could only distance myself from the job – view it through a prism of tolerance, good food, wine, and *caffè corretto* – it might not be so bad. (In other words, become corrupt and lazy like everyone else.)

Perhaps Italy's starting to get to me.

After football yesterday, for no reason other than it was the third half and I was mildly exuberant, I decided to have one last fling at Giulia. I phoned to invite her to dinner, and, surprisingly, she accepted.

I culled the menu entirely from *La Cuisine érotique*, avoiding the more grossly suggestive dishes out of regard for my guest's delicacy of temperament. However, I couldn't resist *Pubis de Crevettes 'Showgirl' aux Doigts d'Avocat* as the starter, partly because of the lurid pun in the title, but mainly because the avocado is, in my humble opinion, the unquestioned nonpareil of erotic fruits. Next came *Cuisses Trompeuses* – the 'deceiving thighs' consisting of artfully laid-out chicken breasts beneath a blanket of cream and white wine sauce, with a small dark cluster of sautéed mushrooms peeping shyly out at the top. For vegetables I plumped unpretentiously for *Carottes à la Façon de l'Ingénieur Khalikiopoulos* (an exceptionally well-endowed Greek civil engineer at the Tsar's court, according to a footnote), *Haricots Verts Enjambés*, and *Pommes de Terre Fesses de la Jolie Levantine.* For dessert a modest *Pêches Péché Cardinal* – again a ghastly pun, but quite exquisite to eat.

Suspecting that Giulia would share her compatriots' absurd ignorance of wine, I chose a nice Cartizze to accompany the meal – sparkling wine being the only kind a lot of young Italians are prepared to drink in any quantity, probably because of its resemblance to their beloved Fanta.

I tidied the flat, put candles on the table, and laid a pile of Ben Webster tapes by the ghetto-blaster. And then – bathed, shaved, groomed, and perfumed – I welcomed Giulia at the door.

She was, as always, most elegantly dressed, somehow avoiding the dreaded middle-aged look that Sarah used to fall into like a heffalump trap whenever she put on anything 'smart'. She simply looked great. She glanced appreciatively at Mrs Cat-eater's antique furniture, admired the view from the window, and seemed unusually relaxed and happy.

All the same, it was hard for me to unwind. I kept thinking of that Ferrari, the box at La Scala, and all the other hints, large and small, that I'd received of her elevated social position. I started to feel that the whole concept of an erotic dinner was indescribably vulgar, and, withdrawing to the kitchen, hastily discomposed my lovingly created prawn and avocado realization of a naughty encounter between lawyer and showgirl.

I immediately regretted it. The result was a bedraggled and melancholy-looking platter – very much *post coitum* – but it was too late.

I took the dish in as it was, muttered something about 'an English hors-d'œuvre', and asked Giulia about her grandmother in Asolo. With tales of this lonely widow we struggled through the first course.

I then asked her about Siena. She looked surprised. I explained that I had phoned while she was away.

'Oh yes. Well . . .' She hesitated slightly. 'My *fidanzato* lives there.'

'Oh. You're to be married?'

'One day. When I qualify. You know how it is. We have to say we're engaged, otherwise we couldn't meet.'

'So you're not officially engaged?'

'No.'

'What does your *fidanzato* do?'

'He works in a bank.'

How amazing, I thought. Just like all the other *fidanzati* of all the other smart young ladies I've met in Pandoro.

I poured more wine and decided it was time for the *Cuisses Trompeuses*. This time, however, I stayed my wrecking hand, and carried in the dish intact.

'Oh!' cried Giulia when she saw it. 'What is it? A fish?'

'No.'

She examined it carefully, and began to laugh.

'Do you find it funny?' I asked.

'Yes . . . Well, no . . . it's so . . . extraordinary.' Her eyes were riveted to it in amazement. 'Did you do this yourself?'

'I did.'

'Really extraordinary . . . It seems a sin to eat such a work of art.'

'It's a labour of love', I said. 'A poem of praise to the beauty of women. And it was made for eating. So eat it. It's no sin.'

'Well,' she said, smiling, 'if you insist', and cut into a soft thigh.

'Oh, this is exquisite,' she said as she tasted it. 'Where do you find the recipe for such incredible food? Not in an English book, I imagine.'

'No. It's a very special book. Do you speak French, by the way?'

'Yes, I do.'

And we were off – no problem.

The evening was a success – I suppose. Giulia seemed to enjoy herself. She drank freely, laughed, and absorbed herself thoroughly in Ubriakov's cuisine. She even liked Ben Webster, or said she did. I lent her a couple of tapes, which she promised to listen to '*senza intellettualizzare troppo*'. Absolutely, I said. Everything went marvellously until the city clocks chimed eleven – a pleasant, distant clangour floating in through the open window, which was brutally interrupted by the doorbell.

'Let's ignore it,' I said.

'No,' she said. 'You can't do that.'

The bell rang again. I went to the entryphone. 'Who is it?'

'Is Giulia there?'

'Who is it?' I repeated.

'Enrico.'

'Wait a moment.' I covered the mouthpiece with my hand. 'It's someone called Enrico for you. Do you know him?'

'My *fidanzato*. I must go.'

'You must go?'

'Yes.'

Feeling somewhat bewildered, I pressed the buzzer to open the downstairs door.

'Has he been waiting in the street in his Ferrari all this time?'

Giulia looked puzzled. 'No. He's been in Vicenza, watching a basketball game.'

'Oh. And where's he taking you now? To a football match?'

'No. A disco. The African Queen.'

'Ah. The African Queen. Of course. Do you always jump up from the dinner table like this?'

Giulia took my hand, and gave me a very straight look. 'Listen, Paul, let's be really clear. I like being with you. You're fun, you're original, you're different. But I've told you, he's my *fidanzato*. Don't start having ideas. If we can be friends, that's wonderful. If not –'

'OK,' I said, feeling twisted with jealousy, trying not to show it. 'That's fine. I understand.' I heard the lift machinery starting to whirr. 'It was great to have you,' I said.

'Thank you, Paul, I enjoyed myself a lot.'

She leaned forward, presenting her cheek for a kiss. I waited a moment, considered a foolhardy attempt on her delicious mouth, and then, as she turned her questioning eyes to me, gave her a chaste kiss on the forehead.

The lift arrived with a thud.

'I will send you an invitation to our *vendemmia*,' she said. 'We pick grapes out on the country estate, then we have a big party with all the peasants.'

'Fine, I'll come and be a peasant too,' I said, and opened the door.

Enrico was standing outside, cold-faced and immaculate in jacket and tie. Giulia introduced me as her English teacher. Wondering why she said this, I shook hands.

'I imagined him older,' he said, addressing Giulia.

She laughed, somewhat falsely. 'Not all teachers are old, you know.'

Enrico wasn't interested. He led her away without another word.

When they had gone, I took a desolate look at the debris of our truncated evening. Serves you right for having desires above your station, I thought; get yourself a Ferrari, peasant, and then go courting Giulias.

And then I thought, hell, life's too short, and went out to Da Marco to get drunk.

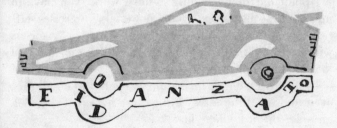

**Monday
30**

Colin is discharged from hospital. I notice, as we leave, he says elaborate goodbyes to the other patients. He's obviously on very friendly terms with them, and has managed to pick up some basic social Italian.

Back home, over coffee, I say, 'Right, Colin, we've got to make some plans', and wave an airline schedule at him.

He says, 'Listen, Paul, I've thought about things a lot. I'd like to stay.'

'Stay? With me? Here?'

'Till I get a place of my own.'

'What will you do for money?'

'Teach English. If it's as easy as you say . . .'

I try to imagine this spiky-haired, black-clad, menacing figure cajoling a class of Pandoro housewives through the minefields of English grammar. The image refuses to come into focus.

'I don't see it somehow, Colin . . . And what about art college? Are you just going to drop that?'

'I'll take a year off.'

'Shouldn't you talk to your tutor first?'

'She'll love the idea. She's always bollocking us for being boring.'

I point out that teaching is hard work; you have to prepare lessons, select your materials, exercise self-restraint, diplomacy, and tact; you must be vigorous without crushing the tender flowers; and – a meaningful look here – you must dress neatly.

He assures me that he is quite prepared to do all this, even to dress differently. 'I'm getting fed up of this look anyway. Bit of a cliché now.'

This astonishing development pleases me. The idea of him staying is worrying, but if it'll help a tormented creature out of his misery, I guess I'm prepared to grit my teeth and put up with it.

Spent all day marking exam papers. Seven hours of surrealism. 'Excuse me, which platform do planes take off from?' 'Are there a hotel room with a good eyesight?' 'What will it cost the fly and the hotel for me and my wife?' 'Please, where is the general interruptor?'

Friday
4

They must have given Colin some amazing efficiency drug at the hospital. He's been out to the shops and bought himself a decent shirt, jacket, and trousers, had a haircut (it still sticks up, but in a tasteful Italian way now), and wangled himself ten hours a week with the gentlemen of the night at the Somerville School. No doubt this was by virtue of being young and male, but still, the important thing is, he's done it. I'm really pleased.

Oral exams begin. These are grim. Crowds of students hover about you in an airless room, feverishly noting down the proceedings, while the unfortunate candidate sits trembling before you, nervous, overdressed, and unable to answer the simplest of questions. You say, 'Right, let's look at "She dwelt among the untrodden ways". Can you tell me what "untrodden" means?'

The student looks at you fearfully for a moment, takes a breath, and unleashes a ghastly flood of fifth-hand bilge out of a potted history about how Wordsworth 'participated to the French Revolution', he was a Romantic, Romantics loved 'the Nature' and believed in 'the Childhood', and how Coleridge and Keats were also Romantics, only they used 'the opium' to have strange visions, Shelley was a revolutionary, Byron an aristocrat, and so on and so forth.

'Yes,' you say, 'that's true – some of it at any rate – but what does the word "untrodden" mean?'

Again the look; a gulp; then, 'Here the poet Wordsworth wants to emphasize the Nature, in which he believes very much.'

'Look,' you say, growing impatient, 'I'm simply asking you to explain the meaning of one word. You don't even need to explain if you don't want to – just translate it.'

The student goes red and frantically consults her notes. 'Untrodden,' she will say. 'Untrodden . . .' Then her face will light up. 'Perhaps it means "difficult"?'

Eventually, to avoid reducing the student to tears, you have to pass on to another question. Then another. And then, when specific questions with specific answers have proved both painful and sterile, you capitulate. 'All right, then, tell me everything you know about Wordsworth and Romanticism.' They immediately relax, and chatter happily for fifteen minutes more about Children, Landscape, Visions, Revolution, and 'the Nature', and you give them a bare pass, and pray for one o'clock to come quickly.

Although most of the students are girls, the prize idiocy of the morning comes from a male. He assures me that 'Tintern Abbey'– all 159 lines of it – is a sonnet.

'Isn't it rather long for a sonnet?'

He looks doubtful. 'Yes,' he says eventually, 'perhaps just a little. But Wordsworth was very experimental . . .'

I'm ashamed to say I passed him – even though the rest of his performance bore similarly eloquent testimony to fantastic ignorance – largely because, in the general repetitiveness and boredom of the occasion, his answers were at least entertaining. It was irresponsible of me, no doubt, but such is our ludicrous (and unchecked) power that we can make the most arbitrary decisions and be sure of getting away with them.

At one o'clock, with buzzing ears and a new loathing for the word 'Nature', we shut up shop and go to the Cacciatore. The litres of *rosso*, the *penne all'arrabbiata*, the meat, salad, and obligatory *caffè corretto* do their customary work, and the afternoon session of exams passes in a timeless digestive haze.

The *vendemmia* on Giulia's family estate. We kick off at nine, with 'corrected coffee' in the courtyard – all the city rich, in their designer gardening clothes, hobnobbing with the hired labourers among tractors, trailers, and baskets. The women sport multicoloured headscarves, which I cynically assume to be a piece of cosmetic 'peasant' costume, until someone informs me that when you're picking grapes a lot of sticky muck comes down off the vines, so it's wise to protect your hair.

We are all issued with secateurs and get harvesting.

You hold a kind of broad-rimmed plastic funnel in your left hand, to catch the grapes which you snip off with your right. When the funnel is full, you tip the grapes into a big basket, or directly into the trailer, which is driven forward a few feet at a time by a rubicund *contadino* in a pork-pie hat.

It's incredibly satisfying work. I was uncomfortably aware at first of social differences – the millionaires playing at wholesome country work among the poor bastards who are condemned to a lifetime of such 'wholesomeness' at dirt-cheap rates – but something in the air makes these feelings quickly evaporate. There is an extraordinary peacefulness and unity about the enterprise, an atmosphere of quiet celebration, even drunkenness. As if the god Bacchus is there among his fruit, blessing the proceedings.

By lunchtime – salami rolls eaten in tearing bites, washed down by gulps of last year's wine from this vineyard – we are all, without the slightest need for explicit statement, like members of the same family. I have the strange and exhilarating feeling of living one of those scenes from a medieval book of hours – scenes which I had always, with the arrogance of those who get their knowledge from books, supposed to be sentimentalized.

I look at Giulia and wonder what she's thinking. She is smiling and wonderfully beautiful. She outshines the autumn sun. I think I'm in love with her. No. I *am* in love with her. I know it's impractical, unreciprocated, and wild, but it's a feeling I can do nothing about. I'm snared.

I even sort of knew when I met her that this was going to happen. That it would be impossible, but somehow necessary.

My mind comes constantly back to Giulia – whatever

I'm doing, wherever I am. Everything reminds me of her: the sun, the rain, flowers on balconies, music, colours, perfumes, the streets leading to her square. When I pass the hospital, I think of her, listening to a lecture somewhere deep in its labyrinth, and I'm envious of her fellow students, the lecturer, even the chair she sits in. I want to be with her, share everything with her, just *see* her.

Can it work? Is there the dimmest chance? Enrico isn't here today. I think about the little lie she told him, about me being her English teacher. On this lie all my hopes depend. It's an implicit acknowledgement that I could be a threat to him – that she could consider me a potential lover. Otherwise surely she might just as well have said I was a friend.

This gives me an idea. Perhaps she really does want English lessons? That would be a perfect way of seeing her, regularly and innocently, without threatening her engagement.

I approach her. 'This has been a wonderful day,' I say.

She seems pleased. 'I knew you'd like it, with your love of wine. It's the best day of the year for everyone . . . We loved it as children too.'

She tells me about a spring that comes out of the hill, on the far side of the vineyard. 'That was a magical place when we were children. We had an old uncle, Lelio, who told us there were tiny gods still living there from antiquity. In the summer we used to stay there for hours, in the shade, waiting for the gods to appear.'

'And did they?'

She laughed. 'Once we thought they did. But it was childish fantasy.'

We walk down the alleys of yellowing vines, out of sight of the others, to a little thicket of birch trees. Giulia points through the shadows to a short, mossy stone pillar, carved with a bearded face. A copper pipe protrudes from its mouth, through which a trickle of clear water flows into a brimming trough. On the trough is written: *'Fabius me fecit. Anno 1563.'*

'Taste the water,' says Giulia. 'It's delicious.'

She bends down to drink, closing her eyes, seeming to dream. As she bends, her shirt falls forward. I turn away, but it's too late. I have already caught a glimpse of her breasts, like two white lilies in the darkness.

'Paul, come and taste . . . What's wrong?'

'Nothing. I think I saw one of the gods.'

She laughs, and comes out of the thicket, her face sparkling with water.

'Come on, Giulia, let's get back. I've seen what I should never have seen.'

'What are you saying?'

I take her hand, and tell her that if we don't go right away I'm in danger – very real danger – of attempting to rape her.

'Oh.' She looks suddenly serious. 'In that case, we'd better go.'

Looking back, I can't help wondering whether she wouldn't have been perfectly happy to be 'raped'. In my rational mind I know this is ridiculous, but the feeling is there, nagging me day and night.

Meanwhile the image of that moment – Giulia leaning forward, those pale, pendulous flowers – stays fixed before me obsessively, burns with inextinguishable fire.

I have a theory – had it since the multiple miseries of student affairs – that the condition of being in love is a virulent disease that paralyses the will and saps the strength. Its only cure is total fulfilment or decisive separation. If you give in to the feeble, floating state of speculative pain, picking petals off daisies and staring moodily out of windows, you're sunk.

There is a third way, which is that of energetic distraction. Getting absorbed, maniacally, in something else. It doesn't work, of course – not for long, anyway – but it provides temporary, harmless relief. This is what I'm opting for now.

I've decided to Make Money. Work Hard and Improve My Condition. Enough of this bohemian mediocrity. I want wealth.

My plan is to do what Bill does: teach business groups. Offer 'Executive English'. That way I can charge forty to fifty thousand lire an hour, and at twenty hours earn a million a week. I need a partner, though.

The obvious choice is Bill – except that he's doing it already, and getting along nicely, thank you. I could also try Rocco, who's got excellent contacts, only I'm afraid he'll be too busy with his painting. The only other person I have the slightest respect for in this oddball expat world is Mike. He's permanently weary, but the glittering rewards may just give him the energy to get off his butt and commit himself.

Saturday 21

Hectic times. Two months without drawing breath. Without a word in the intimate ear of my diary.

Just to catch up, the bare events to date.

Mike and I have started our Executive English scheme, and by dint of much telephoning, massaging, and pestering got ourselves eight hours a week each, divided equally between an animal-feed manufacturer, a drug company, a Coca-Cola concessionaire, and the Association of Pandorese Marble Producers. Thanks to this, I've doubled my income, to two and a half million a month, and I feel really good.

The business world is very, very different from the academic. It's fast, sharp, unforgiving, and much more alert. The fact that people talk about money, instead of abstract words and ideas, in no way compromises the quality of the thought behind the talk. On the contrary. It makes the thought more urgent, penetrating, and decisive.

Working for business also means giving value for money. We have to prepare lessons, tests, reports, etc. with great care. The problem is, the Italians, all Italians, are very lazy students. They love to play you along, make you sloppy and easygoing, and the temptation is to let them get away with it for the sake of a quiet life. But the bosses, who pay for the courses, want results, even if the students don't. So there's always a tension about the work.

Socially, times are thin. Too bushed or busy, bored with the expat scene, I don't go out nearly as much as I used to. A few jaunts with Italian friends take the place of the frequent booze-ups at Da Marco. The usual form is a high-speed drive out to some country restaurant, where we eat till our eyes can scarcely move in their sockets. Conversation is predictable – TV personalities (whom they despise), politicians (ditto, only more so), sport, holidays, and food. No one, it seems, ever reads a book. But the ebullience and *bonhomie* are such that the time passes happily anyway.

Colin has moved out – he shares a flat now with another reformed hooligan down by the university. Whenever I get depressed, I cheer myself up with the thought of the two of them having breakfast together. It never fails to make me laugh out loud and feel grateful for small mercies.

Giulia continues to puzzle (not to say torture) me. Her engagement to Enrico is a dead letter. A formality. But this seems to be precisely what she wants – her 'love life' tucked tidily away in a Siena-registered Ferrari where it won't give her any trouble, leaving her mind free for her studies and the long, meaningless chain of social engagements, occasions – by her own admission – for the display of wealth, poise, and emptiness of mind. When we talk, I sense that she opens out (if you can call anything so cautious 'opening out') as with no one else. Her life is over-regulated and mechanical. Everything, from the marble floors to people's hearts, is polished to an impenetrable glaze.

I know nobody can live like that and be satisfied. I know it's grotesque and false. But I can't break through it – and neither can she. It's all she knows.

My mind goes back to the *vendemmia*, that moment by the spring, and a voice inside me says, 'That was your chance, and you missed it.' I have a feeling of hopelessness. Even if one day, by careful manoeuvring or sheer luck, I could catch her in a similar state of mind, and from that spark of exhilaration light a fire of abandon, how long would it last? What would it destroy of her settled, passionless ways? Nothing, I suspect. I continue to hope for something, some awakening of the heart, but dimly, with little faith.

She started taking English lessons with me in October, but had to stop soon after because of an impending exam. This Christmas she's going skiing with her family, just as she does every year. Enrico will be there, and it'll all be very nice and clockwork as she likes it, and I shall sit here and fume.

Christmas in exile. A group of self-confessed 'old farts' get together to do it the English way, with the traditional dishes of *arrosto di tacchino, cavoli di Bruxelles, salsa di pane,* and *gelatina di mirtilli rossi.* Someone produces a Christmas pudding and a pot of brandy butter, and there's a noisy tripartite division between the 'purists' (just brandy butter), the 'proles' (with custard), and the 'wankers' (who add cream). We quaff gallons of local plonk, there are crackers with silly hats and jokes, charades, and as evening draws on we are hit by a collective attack of nostalgia for the bad old days in Britain, which takes us boozing and fondly remembering long into the small hours.

At 3 am the party staggers out into the fog. It's been a fifteen-hour lunch.

Wednesday
25
Natale di
Gesù

Friday
27

Pandoro empties for the post-Natal Gadarene ski season. I politely decline all invitations to the mountains, and spend my time reading and playing the guitar. Occasional foggy walks. There's talk of a trip to Tuscany, but nothing is certain. It never is.

1986

SEPTEMBER

Sunday 28

Shagger Welsh would be ashamed of me. A whole winter, spring, and summer have passed, and I've recorded nothing.

I made it to Tuscany finally. Not last Christmas, but now, in sweet September – for Giulia's wedding. She and the dreaded Enrico got spliced in Siena Cathedral, a thrilling frame for a sad event – the beautiful Giulia, that live, troubled spirit, clapping on the handcuffs of servitude. *Sic transit gloria mundi.*

I came down for a long weekend with Isabella. We're sort of going out together. She's the complete opposite of Giulia: the daughter of a peasant farmer, raw, red-blooded, undiscriminating, and fun. She was a student of mine – one of the marble magnates' secretaries – who distinguished herself by doing her homework and concentrating in class, thereby actually learning some English. I noticed after a while that she was always among the last to leave the classroom. When this was happening too frequently to be a coincidence, I drew the appropriate conclusion and invited her out for a drink. 'At last!' she said. 'I thought you'd never ask.'

She made her intentions – or at least her availability – totally clear from the start. What amazed me, as we moved inexorably into a 'relationship', was her extraordinary devotion, besottedness almost – even after a couple of nights out. She wanted me, and she was determined to get me and hold on to me.

This caused a problem. As a conquest she was far too easy. Not a 'conquest' at all, in fact.

I like a bit of a chase – a bit of doubt and difficulty. Not as much as Giulia offered, perhaps (she took it to extremes, and it was extremely effective), but at least a challenge. Isabella was a push-over. No contest. One night, in Venice for a concert, we missed the last train home and took a room in a hotel. It was our first real opportunity for naughtiness (she lives with her parents, as they practically all do till they're married), and she leapt into bed with me with the innocent delight of a child jumping into a swimming-pool.

She's generous, uncomplicated, and utterly open. I keep thinking there must be some hidden snake-pit in her soul, which I'll stumble into one day and be devoured. But I see no signs. Everything is straightforward with her. And – hark at this, ye feminists – after making love, she likes to cook me a meal!

I brought her down to Siena as a shock absorber, to take the edge off the pain of seeing Giulia married. It hasn't worked terribly well, though Isabella, of course, is loving it.

We're staying in a room above a bar, just outside the town of Certaldo. It's a 'fine and private place', but unlike Marvell's grave there's a lot of embracing going on, and my mistress is far from coy. Isabella's sitting opposite me on the terrace, reading, while I dawdle with pen and notebook, and hope, by forcing my thoughts through a narrow nib, to give them some much-needed sharpness. I've got some time to think now, and I must use it. To decide what it is exactly that's happened to my life, and what's going to happen next.

I note with distaste that I've become very cynical of late. I think only of pleasure and money. I exploit Isabella, use her endless goodwill, her body, her unquestioning and sympathetic support, purely for my own convenience. I give nothing back. I don't love her – certainly not in the way I loved Giulia, or even Sarah – and doubt if I ever could. If I was honest with her and cared in the slightest for her happiness, I would tell her to go.

My cynicism has not made me happy. In fact it has doubled my unhappiness by adding an element of self-disgust.

I'm also very uncertain about my future in Italy.

Back in England this summer I found myself wanting to stay on. It all started in the unlikely ambience of Folkestone, waiting on the station platform in the sun, watching a family being utterly British near by. The kids raucously claimed to be 'defenders of the universe', their mother was buried in a magazine, smoking Embassies, and the silent grandfather, with his olive-green Terylene trousers, flat cap, and translucent skin, looked on contentedly. It was a very ordinary scene and had nothing special about it at all, except this powerful sense that I had of recognition, a deep, quiet feeling of 'rightness'.

I realized, for the first time, that if I stay in Italy and make my home here, I'll lose all that. That what, precisely? That belonging to something. Which is a crucial thing. Like a knot belongs in a tree, or a blade in a turbine; in its place, its home, with a precise function and purpose. Take it out, it becomes a piece of junk.

That's how I feel right now – like a piece of junk.

So why don't I go back?

For the same reason, I suppose, that I don't tell Isabella to go – convenience. Ease. I make money here. I have an 'enviable lifestyle'. If I go back, I face a totally new beginning, and almost certain unemployment. It would be crazy to leave.

There's a complicating factor, though. While I've been away, by the infallible operation of Sod's Law, a number of my contemporaries have started carving out careers. By sticking to their crummy jobs, they've somehow been spotted and plucked out, and now they're in better jobs, with money and responsibilities and the light of 'belonging' glowing all around them. I can see that I pulled out when the going got rough (or simply dull), sacrificed my future for the sake of a few years in the sun, and now I'm on the scrap-heap.

The question is whether I'm more likely to get off the scrap-heap by staying here or by leaving. I'd like to leave. I'm bored. But is it the right move? Britain's a hostile, competitive environment these days. Italy welcomes me with open arms. How the hell can we see into the future? Or do we just gamble and pray?

Monday 29

Just had one of those glorious Italian days that make you feel privileged to be alive. We walked to San Gimignano, a town of grey medieval towers that looks curiously like New York from a distance. Our panoramic path lay along a ridge, with vineyards undulating across the hills in all directions, and the flame-like twisting cypresses flecked about like exclamation marks punctuating our ecstasy. What splendour! Rapture! And is that a battery-hen shed over there in the distance? No, it can't be! D'you know, it is! Well blow me down!

We had lunch in San Gim, strolled its too-perfectly medieval streets (the place is like a film-set), and set off home again mid-afternoon. On the way back we met an old peasant we recognized from the bar last night. He invited us to his shack in the fields. I thought at first that this was his home, but it turned out to be a store where he keeps his tools, boxes, old bits of unwanted furniture, and a supply of excellent sweet wine. Out the back, the obligatory wheel-less Fiat 500 squats rusting among the olive trees. These are such a standard feature of Italian farms that I suspect there's some kind of EEC grant for them. Perhaps it's the basic qualification for constituting a rural museum.

Our host astounds us by telling us he's eighty; he looks no older than fifty. Either he's lying (but why should he? — perhaps there's another EEC grant involved) or there's something in the air and the wine. You don't see retired London commuters looking like that at eighty.

His name's Leone – Lion. He quotes, with a chuckle, Mussolini's famous piece of drivel: *meglio un giorno da leone che cent'anni da pecora* (better one day as a lion than a hundred years as a sheep).

'That's always struck me as a very bizarre remark,' I say. 'You're either born one or the other.'

'*Eh sì,*' says Leone, and pours more wine.

It was getting dark when we reached our room, both fairly high on the leonine wine. A slight autumn chill frosted the air. Isabella was cold and wanted me to hold her. I did, and we tumbled into bed before supper, and again after a stroll under the stars. She was as happy as a cat by the fireside.

I like her. I like her a great deal. In her quiet way she's very good company, contented, unobtrusive, and easy in herself. I could handle more days like this one, and more with her.

But still something niggles inside me, like a premonition. I feel an urge to escape.

'Please, where is the general interruptor?'

The anniversary of the *vendemmia*. A sad day for me.
Isabella is busy, so I'm left to myself. She's invited me to
her parents' place next weekend for their *vendemmia*. I
know it won't be as good. I'm also trembling because I can
feel it's going to be an 'occasion' for them, when Isabella's
professore is received like a visiting statesman.

What has she told them about me? That we've been out
together. That I'm her *amoroso*? Even (horror of horrors)
that I'm a potential husband? I shudder to think.

I must sort out my thoughts and make some decisions
before then.

Wednesday 15 Met Bill in town and we drank an *aperitivo* together. Talked about business, life in Pandoro, this and that. I said what a shame it was we didn't get together to play football any more. He threw up his shoulders and opened his hands, and said, '*Beh, cosa vuoi? Non c'è tempo.*'

Bill now 'belongs'. That's as clear as day. He's found his place in the machine, and he's whirring around nicely. It struck me that with the destruction and replacement of cells that takes place constantly in our bodies, he must be constructed almost entirely of *pastasciutta* and local wine by now. I shouldn't think there's a British molecule left in him. He's a *de facto* Italian, physically, chemically, and culturally, and it doesn't surprise me when he says he's applied for citizenship.

'You'll have to stop drinking, you know. It'll have to be strictly Fanta from now on.'

'Bollocks,' says Bill with a belch. 'The true Italy is wine. That other stuff will pass away like chaff.'

I ask him how Jane's getting on. I haven't seen her for ages.

'She's gone,' he says. 'Took off with a pilot from Bari.'

'I'm sorry to hear that.'

'Don't be. He's a prize shit, and they suit each other perfectly. It's one less worry on my mind.'

Good old Bill. Tough as an old boot. I still wonder if she told him about us. But perhaps he assumed it anyway.

It's the *vendemmia* tomorrow, and I must decide. My last, desperate attempt to do so. I've been for a walk by the river, sat in a bar, had a bath, paced the room, lain on my back, listened to Ben Webster, made lists of pros and cons, spoken to Mike, Bill, Rocco, and Ferruzzi ('always obey the disruptive element in your life' – whatever that's supposed to mean), and the result of it all is that I'm as undecided as ever.

It was easy ten years ago. There was a Chinese book called the *I Ching*, which it was fashionable to consult like an oracle before deciding anything. I did it myself a few times. Its advice was always sound. You don't see it around any more now, which is a pity. The individual (particularly this individual) is a rotten decision-maker.

I read once (I think in Herodotus) that the Persians used to get drunk before deciding anything. They would then examine their decision in the cold, sober light of the morning, and give it the final go-ahead in a further drunken bout the following evening.

It's mildly consoling to know that Great Civilizations of the Past shared my problem. Their use of dreams, drugs, hallucinations, ravings, trances, riddles, tossed coins, clanking copper pots, clouds, hands, intestines, the flight of birds, and a whole bestiary of similar omens, symbols, and supposed coded messages from the gods shows that they knew a thing or two about indecision themselves.

The only solution I can find is to sleep on it.

**Sunday
19**

The decision is made.

I feel cleaner, stronger, and right about it. But it was dreadful telling Isabella. We'd been picking grapes all day, the sun was shining, the old *vendemmia* magic was there, but it was spoiled for me by the knowledge of what I had to say. I kept putting off the terrible moment. She knew there was something on my mind, and led me off for a walk round the farm to get it out of me.

I told her. She was extremely upset, and at once started to cry.

'I'm sorry,' I said, 'it's stronger than me. It's not you, Isabella, it's Pandoro. Italy. Living here in this luxurious limbo. I don't know who I am any more. I've lost my co-ordinates. I'm in a mess!'

The tears flooded down her cheeks. There was nothing I could say. I felt the complete bastard.

Eventually, with the tears still pouring out of her, she led me to the house and upstairs to her room.

'I want to make love,' she said. 'Even if it's for the last time.' She began undressing.

I hesitated.

'Come on, Paul! Leave me something to remember you by.'

Later, as the light grew dim outside and we lay naked together in her bed, we heard the tractors rolling into the yard and her family returning from the vines.

A door opened downstairs.

'Shouldn't we get up?' I asked.

She shrugged her shoulders. 'It doesn't matter.'

'Your parents will be angry.'

'Let them. I'm not ashamed of my love.' She smiled as she said this, with a confidence and strength in her eyes that made me feel very small, mean, and irrelevant.

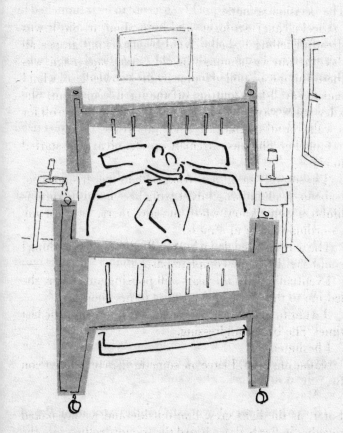

Poor Isabella. She has just introduced me to her parents, slept with me openly beneath their roof – a big step for a good rural Catholic – and now she will have to explain to them why I will never be back.

My conscience condemns me. I should have broken it off earlier or not at all.

Monday 3

I've decided to leave quickly so as not to be trammelled by doubts. Everyone I know is shocked: Mike because our business was going well, Bill because there'll be one less drinker in Pandoro, Rocco because he thinks Italy's paradise and I must have gone off my head.

'Take a break, man, go to Napoli, Sicilia, go to Gubbio. Take a weekend in Rome.'

'No, Rocco, I don't need any more holidays, I just need to touch home base.'

'What the hell for?'

'I don't know. Just to do it. I feel the need.'

'OK, go home for a few weeks. Take the cure, whatever it is. But don't burn your boats.'

'They're already burnt.'

He shakes his head. 'Your affairs – everything?'

'My affairs – both amorous and financial – are wound up.'

'What about Isabella? You're leaving her here?'

'Yes.'

'I don't believe it.'

'Come on, Rocco! What could she do in England? She's a typist. Her English isn't good enough to get work.'

'She'd find work. She's smart.'

'Maybe.'

Rocco looks very downcast. 'You're crazy, man. *Pazzo.*'

I find his concern strangely moving. Sometimes it's only when you say goodbye to a person that you realize how important they are to you. Rocco's been fun to know. I shall miss him.

Getting out of the Italian bureaucracy is every bit as difficult as getting in. I try to close my bank account by the relatively straightforward process of going into the bank and saying, 'Please close my account.' The clerk tells me it's impossible. I need letters, certificates of transferred residence and termination of contract, statements of this and that, notarized declarations, documents stamped by the municipality – everything, in fact, bar a blood sample and a plaster cast of my teeth. 'That's ridiculous,' I tell him. 'I'm leaving the country. I'm making no further transactions on this account. For all practical purposes it's dead. If the bank wants to waste money sending statements to my old address, that's their problem.' He smiles politely, and says, 'I'm sorry, but without the proper documents I cannot close your account.' And so I leave it, as everything is left in this zany land, to the tender care of inertia.

This experience teaches me to avoid even contacting the municipal authorities, the police, and the tax office. I haven't got time to waste. I shall simply depart and leave them to draw the appropriate conclusions.

Wednesday 12

Everything's ready. I'm sitting in my cleaned-up, packed-up apartment, looking out over the familiar view of bell-towers, domes and rooftops, a view I've seen through every season and degree of alcoholic intoxication and hangover, through mists and fogs, rain, snow, hail, and blazing sun, a view that's been my companion for almost three years. In a few minutes we must part. In the building opposite I can see the loony housewife who hoovers her balcony every morning, and I guess I shall have to do

without her too. Sounds of the street come floating up: the buzzing of Vespas, the squawking of two fur-coated ladies inquiring after their husbands' healths, the bread delivery-man grunting into entryphones. It's going to be hard to leave the daily comedy of Italian life, its essential sweetness, and go back to the harshness of Britain. But I've got to do it. You can't eat lotus for ever.

I rang Isabella this morning, to 'salute' her, as they say here, and apologize for everything. She was calm and cheerful and told me not to be remorseful. She had gone into it all with her eyes open, she said, and I was not to blame. She said she loved me, and didn't know when she would be able to love anyone else. 'You must try,' I said, and she agreed that in the end perhaps this was a good idea.

I still marvel at her good character, her incredible lack of ill will. She's one in a million.

Saturday 15	Finsbury Park. Blustery showers and cloud. The all-strangling traffic. *Quest'isola grigia senza stagioni.* I'm back.

I have everything to do. Find work, accommodation, a rhythm of life. My parents invited me to stay with them — they'd love it, of course (so they say), but it would soon become a strain, then a nightmare, and finally a horror story. So I'm staying with Paddy Colston. His flatmate's away in Australia.

Despite the much-bruited Thatcher-induced unemployment, there are plenty of jobs advertised, and I'm hoping to get fixed up soon. There's always good old English teaching if things get dire — but I could do with a break from that.

Immediate impressions of London: less obviously 'depressing' than I expected, though there are madmen, roughnecks, and drunks in abundance; the roads dirtier than I remember, and very busy; the weather like a lid on your thoughts.

Decided to ring up a few language schools to check pay, hours, their need for teachers, etc. Horrified to hear that the 'standard rate' is five pounds an hour. (Compare that with the fifteen to twenty pounds I was getting in Pandoro, where the cost of living's lower.) Advertisements in the press offer salaries of six to nine thousand pounds for responsible, difficult jobs. How anyone can *live* on that, rather than merely subsist, beats me. The minimum necessary for a decent way of life seems to be more like twice that.

Sunday 23	Today I made the mistake of re-reading the start of my Italian diary. It seems incredible now how vigorous and optimistic I felt. Full of the joys of discovery. Cocky and bright. I wish I felt the same about returning to Britain. My experience has closed in on itself. I've come full circle. Only I don't feel as if I'm quite the same me that set out three years ago. If anything, I've gone down a notch or two, down a ring in the spiral. And the fruit of my wanderings has been nothing more than to come home in a more battered condition than when I left.

I tell myself there must have been gains – in experience, knowledge of human nature, knowledge of myself perhaps – but the gains don't seem to translate at all into anything usable in England. I've learned life skills that work in Italy. I'm reminded that my home is an island, and they do things differently here.

There's an Italian café round the corner, where they serve the London version of cappuccino: two parts Thames water to one part boiling milk, squirted at high pressure through a piece of brown paper with the word 'coffee' scrawled on it. A travesty. The proprietors are a nice middle-aged couple from Benevento; cheery enough, but you can tell they've been beaten by life. Their skin is grey and their eyes tired. They've succumbed to that reduced expectation of happiness that's integral to the British way of life. They came here thirty years ago, and all the progress they've made is from the squalor of southern Italy in the fifties to the squalor of London in the eighties. If they'd stayed at home, they'd probably be rich by now.

I hate to say this, but I'm still restless. The excitement of being back has worn off with incredible speed and I'm starting to wonder what I'm doing here. I suppose this was to be predicted. Once you've tasted the pleasure of abroad, that sense of freedom, it's hard to be content with the prospect of the same familiar scenes (and what scenes!) for the next forty years. I met expats with this problem in Pandoro. They'd lived in four or five different countries, and couldn't be happy in any of them. They were always obsessed with the thought that life might be better somewhere else. I can see myself going that way too if I'm not careful.

Except that I do actually *want* to settle down and achieve something. I've come round, in a sense, to Sarah's point of view: the need for a 'career'. The question remains, though: am I really interested in doing it in Britain, where the distance between drudgery and reward is so oppressively vast?

There's an ad in the paper for English-language instructors in Saudi Arabia. Eighteen thousand pounds a year, tax free. I'm going to apply.

Tuesday 25	Down to Winchester for a few days to stay with Mum and Dad. They're so happy I'm back, it almost hurts. They write off my years in Italy as an aberration, a temporary sickness from which I'm now fully recovered. I find this more than a little insulting, but have no stomach for fights just now.

Had an odd 'episode' this morning. After scouring the newspaper for jobs, I went out for a run. Came back feeling very strange indeed: wobbly on my legs, dizzy, totally drained of energy. I lay down, but only felt worse. My chest seemed to be tightening by the minute, as if the front and back were being screwed together. I grew short of breath. My hands felt like lumps of ice. Dad called the doctor, and must have given her a scare, because she came running.

She checked my pulse, blood pressure and heart, and said there was nothing wrong. 'You seem perfectly healthy to me.'

'I don't feel it,' I said.

'How do you feel?'

'Horrible.'

Then she asked me what I was doing these days. I told her. She listened carefully, thought about it a bit, and said, 'Well, I'd say you're depressed.'

This came as a shock. 'You mean Depressed? With a capital D?'

'That's right.'

'I don't feel depressed . . . A bit fed up perhaps, but nothing serious. Nothing clinical.'

'That could be the problem. You're intelligent, you see, and you can put on an act —'

'An act? Who for?'

'For everyone. Including yourself.'

She was a tough cookie, this one. No nonsense about her. One of the old breed of family doctors who give it to you straight from the shoulder. But I was suspicious of this so-called 'Depression'.

I asked her if she was sure. She said of course she couldn't be, but she was quite certain there was nothing wrong with me physically. 'All the same, you ought to see your GP in London.'

'I haven't got one.'

She frowned. 'Then you must find one. It's important to get this seen to.'

She left, shrugging off Dad's effusive thanks.

I thought about it. My first reaction was to think she was dispensing the current flavour-of-the-decade stuff. In Italy they tell you to get a blood test, in the States they fill you with vitamins, in Britain they tell you you're depressed. It's a way of getting you off their hands. But then I noticed that I did actually feel much better; the symptoms had disappeared just by talking about it. So perhaps she's right after all.

Thursday 27

London. Went into the local surgery to sign up with a doctor. A cramped subterranean waiting-room, packed with snuffling patients. It felt like a vestibule to the halls of the dead.

The nurse at the desk offered me an appointment in eight days.

'Nothing sooner than that?'

'Not unless it's an emergency, I'm afraid.'

It's scarcely that, so I accept.

Out in the street, with a fresh wind blowing, I feel perkier. But beneath it all I am depressed, there's no two ways about it. Somewhere along the line I've lost my hope.

Back in Paddy's flat I go through the paper for jobs. Nothing.

Then I get a bright idea. I'll ring Sarah. Perhaps we could get together for a meal. I dig out her office number and dial. The secretary casually tosses me a bombshell. Sarah's away. 'Oh yes, where?' 'On honeymoon.' 'Thank you,' I say. I can guess the rest.

For want of anything more pressing to do, I have a bath and wash my hair. Afterwards, in the mirror, I notice that I've somehow managed, in the space of a few weeks, to start looking old. There are heavy lines around my mouth, pouches under my eyes, and, over my ears, the first insidious grey hairs. I'm tempted to pull them out – but what's the point? It's like killing the messenger that brings bad news.

In the nicest possible way (the Civil Service does a good job) Paddy tells me his flatmate returns on Wednesday, and I should be thinking about 'alternative arrangements'. This further blackens my mood. I go out to the Italian café. Not for their dreadful cappuccino – just to hear them speak Italian.

DECEMBER

Monday
1

Back down to Winchester. With money running out, it's my only option. The approach of Christmas gives a gloss of plausibility to this essentially defeatist move. I don't want to live in Winchester, the place means nothing to me. But there's a free bed, and all the food I can eat – which doesn't seem to be much these days.

Something's wrong. Very deeply and horribly wrong. I can't put my finger on it, but I feel as if I'm being whirled, slowly but inevitably, down into a vile, black, stinking drain. My mother can sense it, and I catch a look of pity in her eyes in unguarded moments, which she tries to cover up with a smile. Dad probably senses it too, but dismisses it. God, for a dash of his blunt cheerfulness!

What is it? Failed expectations? Disappointment with myself? My nerve gone?

It's as if I left something vital of myself in Italy. Like a bee that leaves its sting behind, and, in attempting to fly away, tears out half its insides.

But perhaps leaving Italy was just coincidental. Perhaps this was coming to me anyway.

I found myself wandering towards the cathedral this afternoon, and took the opportunity to go in and – I'm half ashamed to admit it – pray. If God exists, I thought, this would be a very effective time to show His hand.

I prayed, awkwardly, for myself, and by extension for all the other people on earth who are going through pain. I also prayed for all the losers and idiots I've met over the years (because I feel I'm one of them?), for my parents, and for all the friends I left behind in Italy. For Isabella too, who rests most uneasily on my conscicence.

Praying is hard work. There are so many people to think of. If you were thorough, you'd never stop. And it's complicated by the fact that you don't know whether you're doing the most important thing in the whole of existence or merely being a fool.

Evensong started, and I sat through it. Went out into the dusk feeling marginally better – whether by exposure to words of hope, or by something more mysterious, I wouldn't know.

Wednesday 3 Read the paper, and supped full with horrors. For some reason violence and brutality to children, even new-born infants, seems to have become fashionable in this country. Soon we'll be looking back to the days of armed bank robberies and conventional murder with nostalgia.

Had a walk with Dad in the afternoon, down by the Itchen. Mild, sunny weather. He asked what my plans are. I found it hard to answer. 'Just to get through this day,' I felt like saying, 'then think about getting through tomorrow.' What I did say in the end was, 'Wait and see.'

'Wait for what?'

'I don't know. Something'll turn up.'

He grunted. 'What about the Job Centre? Been down there yet?'

His tone, as well as the question itself, disturbed me.

'No,' I said. 'I haven't been to the Job Centre, because I don't want to work in Winchester, and in any case they don't have jobs for teachers and ex-editors of building trade manuals.'

'Oh. I thought they had all kinds.'

'No.'

Not a very useful conversation, but it's about as far as I can go with Dad at the moment.

Just realized with a jolt that I've missed my doctor's appointment in London. Didn't phone or anything. This annoys me – the lapse of memory more than missing the doctor. Still, I doubt if it would have been much help. I need a job, a role in life – not pills.

**Saturday
6**

A letter from Isabella this morning. She's pregnant. This is absolutely the last thing I need.

What a bloody awful weekend. Me feeling dreadful about
Isabella – she wants to know whether to keep the child, I
don't know what to say, what to think – the atmosphere in
the house drifting by perceptible degrees towards a major
barometric Low. Mum and Dad have quite clearly
guessed that things are going anything but well for me,
and the air is heavy with unspoken, unspeakable
thoughts.

    Meanwhile the record of actual words exchanged over
the past few days would fit comfortably on to a small
telegram.

Thursday 11

Up to London for my first interview. The Saudi job. A couple of tanned 'executives' (i.e. jumped-up English teachers in suits) question me earnestly about classroom techniques, progress assessment, and what differences I would expect between working in Italy and Saudi Arabia.

'Well, for a start, you can't drink in Saudi,' I say, 'so there's less chance of being pissed in lessons.'

They look at me stonily. 'Do you drink?'

'Never,' I say.

One of them writes something down, and we pass on to the enthralling matter of the role of the video recorder in English-language teaching.

They strike me as a dreary lot — my fellow hopefuls as much as the interviewers — and the temptation is small. But the money . . . it's too good to ignore. If they offer, I shall probably accept — even though it's a minimum two-year contract. What have I got to lose?

Dragged out of bed by a nine o'clock phone-call to say I've got the job. They want me to go to an 'induction meeting' on Wednesday. This lifts my mood considerably (it's nice to feel wanted, even by mediocrities), though a slight edge of doubt remains about plunging off into Arabia Non-Alcoholica quite so blithely.

I'm also worried about Isabella. I keep replaying scenes from our time together – the bar near Certaldo, Mr Lion's shack in the fields, a hotel-room in Venice, her parents' farm, and us, making love at every opportunity, laughing and drinking – why the hell did I leave her? Do I *ever* get anything right?

Saturday 20

A passable, busy week. Spent some time at the public library, reading about Saudi. Its wealth and repressive laws. I doubt if I would choose to go there on holiday.

The induction meeting went smoothly enough – full of talk about 'aggressive language targeting', 'ongoing profile definition', 'holistic programme development goals', and similar pseuderies, which we all nodded at sagely without believing a word. The salary, leave arrangements, health care, etc. all sounded fine, but I was a little put off by the description of the accommodation as 'single-sex compounds, with grade-related recreational facilities'. (One's 'grade' is apparently determined by one's nationality. So why don't they say 'nationality'?)

We will be expected to work forty-four hours a week – twenty-four teaching and twenty administration. They want their pound of flesh all right – but from what I've heard, there's not much to do out there anyway except work.

They gave me a contract to sign, which I said I would like to take home and read. At this they bristled. Why didn't I read it there and then, it was just standard formalities, and couldn't I see everyone else was signing? The psychological pressure was fairly hefty, but it only made me more determined to resist. I told them I never sign anything without reading it extremely carefully first.

'You'd better not hang around,' they said. 'We have plenty of applicants waiting.'

Last posting day before Christmas, and I still haven't sent off the contract. Do I really want to go to Saudi Arabia, I ask myself, and knock out two years of my life for the sake of, say, ten thousand pounds more than I could get either here or somewhere civilized in Europe? Somewhere with bars, theatres, and music? What's the point?

And then, with this festival going on all around me, ostensibly to celebrate the birth of a child, I feel guilty all over again about Isabella. I still haven't replied to her letter or called her. All I've done is dither.

I can't make up my mind. I'll decide over Christmas (I've got to) and drop the contract in by hand.

Christmas Day	For lunch we trundle off to Uncle Peter's down at Lymington. There in the front room, with its window sprayed with fake snow, among the presents and cards and smells of roasting turkey, sits an incredibly well-scrubbed and contented-looking Colin.

For some reason I didn't expect to find him here.

He jumps up. 'Really good to see you, Paul. Really good. I wasn't sure I'd make it, but I just managed to get on to a flight from Treviso at the last minute, so here I am!'

Auntie Betty and Uncle Peter grin. The great embarrassment of their lives – they didn't talk to him for five years in his Camberwell phase – has turned into a golden boy. South African sherry is poured. 'Welcome home, both of you,' says Uncle Peter, raising his glass.

After lunch and The Queen, Colin suggests a walk. The old duffers sleepily decline, so it's just us. We go down to the sea, where a warm, damp wind is blowing.

Colin makes me uncomfortable almost immediately by saying he wants to thank me for all I did for him, and 'well, basically, for saving my life'. I remind him it was the firemen of Pandoro who did this.

'No, I mean the support you gave me. Before and after.'

'That was the least I could do,' I tell him.

'No,' he says, 'you cared, you gave me the time of day.'

I want to change the subject. 'How's it going in Italy?' I ask.

'Great,' he says. 'Loving it . . . How's England?'

'Not so great. I'm leaving.'

He's surprised – then astonished when I tell him where I'm going. I explain the advantages – or rather the advantage – of the Saudi job. I try to make it sound positive, hoping to convince myself.

'There's no wine in Saudi Arabia,' says Colin.

I wince. 'Don't remind me. I'm trying not to think about it.'

Back at the house, over tea and Auntie Betty's Himalayan Christmas cake, the conversation turns to Italy.

'What do they do out there at Christmas?' asks Uncle Peter.

'Same as us. Eat, drink, get together.'

'Do they give presents?'

'Oh yes.' Colin is quite the expert. 'Only they don't eat turkey. Not for Christmas. It's the cheapest meat you can buy, you see, so it's not special like it is here.'

'What do they eat, then? Spaghetti?' Uncle Peter finds this hilarious and rocks with laughter. He has to put his cup of tea down on a side-table for fear of spilling it.

'They have spaghetti first, or some other form of pasta, then three or four different meats.'

'Oh!' says Auntie Betty, raising her eyebrows. 'Very grand!'

'I thought they were poor,' says Mum. 'Do they kill their own animals?'

'No. They go to the butcher's like anyone else. And they're not poor. They're a lot better off than we are, if their clothes and cars are anything to go by.'

'D'you think you'll make a go of it out there?' asks Dad.

'Reckon I might,' says Colin. 'It's got everything I want.'

'How about painting?' I ask. 'Doing any of that?'

'Not just at the moment. But I'm going to start when I get a bigger flat. My first target's a car, though. Then I can really enjoy life – steam out to the lake, the mountains . . .'

Uncle Peter shakes his head. 'You know, Colin, when I think what you were like before you went out there . . .' Colin tries to object, but his father goes on: 'unwashed, unhealthy, all bad language and that horrible greasy punk hair . . . We were ashamed of you, weren't we, Betty?'

She crinkles up her nose at the memory, as if a bad smell had invaded the room.

'And then I look at you now, the way you've come back, a decent young man, smart, good-mannered, and I think you've got to hand it to the Italians. They've got something we haven't . . .' He leans back in his chair and crosses his stubby legs. 'I mean, what is it that's gone wrong with Britain? Can either of you lads tell me? Paul?'

I look at the floor. I hate this kind of conversation. 'I wish I knew . . . I suppose it may be something to do with the great cycles of history – empires grow, flourish, then decay, just as people do. You can't fight it. It's just the way things are.'

'Ah, but is it?'

No one seems to know, and the conversation fizzles out.

Auntie Betty offers more tea and cake while Uncle Peter prods the fire. Someone notices that Dad has fallen asleep and his mouth is hanging open. Mum goes over and shuts it for him.

At home in the evening we watch a hopeless 'comedy' show on TV. Even Mum and Dad, whose standards are pretty undemanding, seem bored. Melancholy settles over us. Sadness grips my heart.

I ask Dad if I can phone Italy. He looks surprised, as if I'd shaken him from a dream. 'I'll pay,' I say.

I go into the hall and dial the number, my decision flickering inside me like a candle in a draughty room.

We're connected. It begins to ring.

The ringing goes on for ages.

Please, someone, be in, I'm thinking. I don't know when I'll reach such a point of decisiveness again. By tomorrow I may have changed my mind . . .

Suddenly it's picked up. '*Pronto?*' a sleepy voice answers.

'Isabella? Is that you?'

Wednesday 31

Colin and I arrived at Gatwick at 6.30 yesterday evening, picked our way to the check-in through an enormous crowd of skiers, only to be told that due to fog in northern Italy and snow everywhere else there'd be an 'indefinite delay'. 'Infinite' would have been more to the point.

Now at last, fourteen hours later, bleared, bored, and sleepless, we're up; coffee's being served, and I'm looking out of the window at a white Europe below. Just ahead, where the perspex thickens and distorts the view, I catch a first glimpse of the Alps.

It's a sight that always lifts my heart – like a door into a new world.

FOR THE BEST IN PAPERBACKS, LOOK FOR THE 🐧

In every corner of the world, on every subject under the sun, Penguin represents quality and variety – the very best in publishing today.

For complete information about books available from Penguin – including Puffins, Penguin Classics and Arkana – and how to order them, write to us at the appropriate address below. Please note that for copyright reasons the selection of books varies from country to country.

In the United Kingdom: Please write to *Dept E.P., Penguin Books Ltd, Harmondsworth, Middlesex, UB7 0DA.*

If you have any difficulty in obtaining a title, please send your order with the correct money, plus ten per cent for postage and packaging, to *PO Box No 11, West Drayton, Middlesex*

In the United States: Please write to *Dept BA, Penguin, 299 Murray Hill Parkway, East Rutherford, New Jersey 07073*

In Canada: Please write to *Penguin Books Canada Ltd, 2801 John Street, Markham, Ontario L3R 1B4*

In Australia: Please write to the *Marketing Department, Penguin Books Australia Ltd, P.O. Box 257, Ringwood, Victoria 3134*

In New Zealand: Please write to the *Marketing Department, Penguin Books (NZ) Ltd, Private Bag, Takapuna, Auckland 9*

In India: Please write to *Penguin Overseas Ltd, 706 Eros Apartments, 56 Nehru Place, New Delhi, 110019*

In the Netherlands: Please write to *Penguin Books Nederland B.V., Postbus 195, NL–1380AD Weesp*

In West Germany: Please write to *Penguin Books Ltd, Friedrichstrasse 10–12, D–6000 Frankfurt/Main 1*

In Spain: Please write to *Longman Penguin España, Calle San Nicolas 15, E–28013 Madrid*

In Italy: Please write to *Penguin Italia s.r.l., Via Como 4, I-20096 Pioltello (Milano)*

In France: Please write to *Penguin Books Ltd, 39 Rue de Montmorency, F-75003 Paris*

In Japan: Please write to *Longman Penguin Japan Co Ltd, Yamaguchi Building, 2–12–9 Kanda Jimbocho, Chiyoda-Ku, Tokyo 101*